A Word from Stephanie
about Finding an Older Brother

My best friends Darcy, Allie, Kayla and I were sitting at our regular lunch table, with our regular lunch crew, when Jennifer, one of our classmates, walked into the cafeteria.

Everyone noticed that since school started, something was different about her. She started wearing some really cool clothes—and started acting in a really uncool way. Every chance she got, Jennifer put me down!

If I mentioned that I saw a cool movie last weekend, Jennifer saw one that was cooler. If I talked about the hot new outfit I bought at the mall, Jennifer bought one that was much hotter.

I couldn't help but wonder what her problem was. Why was Jennifer trying to make herself look better than me in front of all our friends? Then Allie came up with the answer. Jennifer was trying to become one of the most popular girls in school. The problem was, she thought she had to make *me* look bad to do it!

Totally ridiculous, right? I ignored Jennifer at first, but then her put-downs became so nasty, I couldn't let them go anymore. That's when the *real* trouble started.

Jennifer started bragging about her older brother. And I really wanted to give her a taste of her own medicine. So—before I knew what I was doing, I told everyone I had an "older brother" too. A foreign exchange student who was coming to stay with me and my family. I told everyone that my older brother was better then Jennifer's. In fact, *Jean-Pierre* was incredibly cute, smart, talented—and *French!*

It worked! Everyone believed I had a cool older brother. That is, everyone except Jennifer. She challenged me to prove that this amazing guy existed.

Yikes! Now I have to find an older brother—a cute, smart, French-speaking one—before everyone finds out the truth—and Jennifer has the last laugh!

Not that I *need* an older brother. Our house is practically *overflowing!* Right now, there are nine people and a dog living there. And for all I know, someone new could move in at any time. There's me, my big sister, D.J., my little sister, Michelle, and my dad, Danny. But that's just the beginning. When my mom died, Dad needed help. So he asked his old college buddy, Joey Gladstone, and my Uncle Jesse to come live with us, to help take care of me and my sisters.

Back then, Uncle Jesse didn't know much about taking care of three little girls. He was more into rock 'n' roll. Joey didn't know anything about kids, either—but it sure was funny watching him learn!

Having Uncle Jesse and Joey around was like having three dads instead of one! But then something even better happened—Uncle Jesse fell in love. He married Rebecca Donaldson, Dad's co-host on his TV show, *Wake Up, San Francisco*. Aunt Becky's so nice—she's more like a big sister than an aunt.

Next, Uncle Jesse and Aunt Becky had twin baby boys. Their names are Nicky and Alex, and they are adorable!

I love being part of a big family. Still, things can get pretty crazy when you live in such a full house!

FULL HOUSE™: Stephanie novels

Phone Call from a Flamingo
The Boy-Oh-Boy Next Door
Twin Troubles
Hip Hop Till You Drop
Here Comes the Brand-New Me
The Secret's Out
Daddy's Not-So-Little Girl
P.S. Friends Forever
Getting Even with the Flamingoes
The Dude of My Dreams
Back-to-School Cool
Picture Me Famous
Two-for-One Christmas Fun
The Big Fix-up Mix-up
Ten Ways to Wreck a Date
Wish Upon a VCR
Doubles or Nothing
Sugar and Spice Advice
Never Trust a Flamingo
The Truth About Boys
Crazy About the Future
My Secret Secret Admirer
Blue Ribbon Christmas
The Story on Older Boys
My Three Weeks as a Spy
No Business Like Show Business
Mail-Order Brother

Club Stephanie

#1 Fun, Sun, and Flamingoes
#2 Fireworks and Flamingoes
#3 Flamingo Revenge
#4 Too Many Flamingoes
#5 Friend or Flamingo?
#6 Flamingoes Overboard!

Available from MINSTREL Books

FULL HOUSE™
Stephanie

Mail-Order Brother

Laura O'Neil

A Parachute Book

PUBLISHED BY POCKET BOOKS
New York London Toronto Sydney Tokyo Singapore

A MINSTREL PAPERBACK *Original*

 A Minstrel Book published by
POCKET BOOKS, a division of Simon & Schuster Inc.
1230 Avenue of the Americas, New York, NY 10020

A PARACHUTE BOOK

 Copyright © and ™ 1998 by Warner Bros.

FULL HOUSE, characters, names and all related indicia are trademarks of Warner Bros. © 1998.

ISBN: 0-671-01726-8

First Minstrel Books printing September 1998

10 9 8 7 6 5 4 3 2 1

A MINSTREL BOOK and colophon are registered trademarks of Simon & Schuster Inc.

Cover photo by Schultz Photography

Printed in the U.S.A.

Mail-Order Brother

CHAPTER
1

◆ ◀ ◣ ◆

"Come on, Allie, what is it?" Stephanie Tanner leaned across the cafeteria table toward her best friend, Allie Taylor. "What is this big surprise?"

Allie sat between two of Stephanie's other close friends—Darcy Powell, a tall, pretty girl with long black curls and smooth brown skin, and Maura Potter, who had hazel eyes and long straight dark hair.

Allie's green eyes shone with excitement. She twirled a strand of her light brown hair and gazed up at the ceiling. She was obviously enjoying the game of teasing them with her secret.

"You're driving us crazy with these little hints

1

you've been dropping all day," Darcy added. "Tell us already."

"Enough mystery," Maura agreed.

"All right," Allie finally gave in. "Wait until you hear this. You won't believe it."

The three friends leaned in closer. The long table where they were sitting was crowded with their usual group of ninth-grade girls.

"Okay," Allie began. "The reason I didn't tell you all before is that it wasn't definite. But now it is. My parents got the letter of confirmation yesterday afternoon. There's finally going to be a brother in my house. Next week!"

"Your mother's having a baby?" Stephanie squealed. Her blue eyes lit up with happiness. Allie was an only child. Stephanie, who came from a big family, always thought that it must be terribly lonely for her friend.

"Wait a minute," Stephanie said, frowning. "I saw your mother yesterday. She looked the same as always. There's no way she could have a baby next week."

"Very true," Allie agreed with a giggle.

"I know," Stephanie said. "Your parents are adopting one!"

Allie shook her head and laughed. "No, you're totally off."

"Explain, then," Darcy demanded with a frustrated sigh.

"A boy from France is going to live with us for a month," Allie told them. "He's sixteen and right now he lives in Paris. He's staying with us as part of a foreign exchange program. My parents volunteered us to be a host family and put up a student for a month. Then someone in France will do the same for me when I'm sixteen."

"Wow! It will be like you really have an older brother," Stephanie said. "At least for a while."

"How totally cool," Maura said. "A guy from Paris! Parisians are so sophisticated. No one else dresses the way they do." Maura, who was into vintage clothing, had an eye for fashion.

"I love the way they talk," Darcy said. *"Bonjour, ma chérie . . ."*

"I bet he'll be a real hunk," Stephanie whispered. "All French guys are. I bet you and he will fall in love, Allie. And after you write each other really passionate letters for a few years, he'll return and take you back to Paris with him."

"No way!" Allie said, laughing. "Steph, he's going to be living with us, like part of the family—like a brother. You can't date someone who's like your brother!"

"Good!" Darcy's dark eyes twinkled. "Then I can date him. He won't be *my* brother."

"You're all crazy," Maura said, rolling her eyes. "He's not even here yet. You don't know anything about him. Whether he's nice or obnoxious—"

"I know his name," Allie said. "It's Jean-Pierre."

A loud voice at the other end of the lunch table caught Stephanie's attention.

"He was beyond gorgeous—he was magnificent!" Jennifer James told a group of girls who sat listening intently to her.

Justine Murphy, who sat beside her, smiled. "I saw him once. You're right. He's way beyond gorgeous!"

Allie's eyes met Stephanie's. "Whoa! Who are they talking about?" she whispered.

Stephanie shrugged and glanced down the table. Jennifer had changed so much since last year that Stephanie hardly recognized her.

Last year, in eighth grade, Jennifer was quiet, average—the type no one really noticed. She came back from summer vacation changed, though. Her long brown hair was now styled in a sharp, chin-length cut. She wore contact lenses instead of glasses, and she had a whole new wardrobe.

Darcy leaned closer and spoke in a whisper. "You know, I thought we were friends with Jennifer. But every time I've tried to talk to her this year, she looks at me and says, 'Later, Darce.' Like I'm not worth talking to."

Stephanie thought back. She and Jennifer weren't close friends, but they had chatted in study hall and helped each other with their science homework. That was last year. She had tried to talk to Jennifer a few times since school began, and, like Darcy, she was brushed off each time.

"He must have been hard to handle," Gia Mactavish said to Jennifer.

"Not at all. He was magnificent. In absolutely every way."

Stephanie couldn't help it. It was too intriguing to ignore. She had to jump in. "Magnificent?" she echoed. "Sounds like a pretty unusual guy."

The smile faded from Jennifer's face. "I'm not talking about a *guy*," she said disdainfully. "I was speaking about the most magnificent horse on earth. I rode him this summer at the Stoneridge Horse Farm, where I took lessons."

"He's a Thoroughbred," Alexa Martin added.

Stephanie felt a little embarrassed about her mistake. "Oh! It's so cool to take riding lessons," she said. "I rode a little last Christmas. I loved it and—"

"Anyway, as I was saying, this horse was wonderful." Jennifer cut Stephanie off. She turned to Amber Pierce and Laura Cohen, who were sitting near her, turning her back on Stephanie and her friends. "I rode him so well that after two weeks they offered me a position as a junior instructor at the farm."

Stephanie sat back in her seat, stunned. "What was that about?" she asked her friends. "I was just trying to be friendly and make conversation."

"I don't know," Maura said. "But she really shut you down fast, and now she's ignoring all of us."

"I guess she didn't want anyone stealing her spotlight," Darcy suggested in a low, irritated voice.

"She's been shooting all of us down—especially *you*, Stephanie—ever since school started," Allie added. "Haven't you noticed?"

Stephanie nodded. "I thought maybe I was imagining things or being too sensitive."

"Trust me, you're not," Darcy said.

"It's definitely real," Allie agreed. What's with her? She used to be nice. This year, though, I've seen her do all sorts of snotty things. The other day she was trashing a girl in the locker room just because her socks didn't match."

"Ouch." Maura winced. "I remember what it feels like to be on the receiving end of that." Maura, who had a unique style, used to be teased and shunned until Stephanie and her friends got to know how cool she really was.

Stephanie tightened the scrunchie in her long blond hair. "Jennifer and I were never that close, but we were never enemies, either," she said. "I just don't get why she's suddenly so hostile."

Darcy took a last sip of her juice. "I say she's jealous."

"What's she got to be jealous of?" Stephanie asked. "She's pretty, she's smart . . . I don't get it."

"You're prettier, smarter, and more popular," Allie said loyally. "She seems determined to be Miss Popularity. Maybe she thinks she needs to seem better than us to become more popular."

"If that's true, it's really dumb," Stephanie replied. "And whatever the reason, it's getting on my nerves."

"Maybe she doesn't realize what she's doing," Allie suggested. She tilted her head thoughtfully. "You know what? Maybe if you *show* her how annoying she's being, she'll get the idea and lay off you."

Stephanie propped her chin on her hand to consider Allie's suggestion. "How can I show her how she's acting? I don't want to act as obnoxiously as she does," she decided.

"I don't know what else you can do to get her to stop," Allie insisted.

"I think it's a good idea," Darcy said. "Someone's got to show her she's behaving like a total creep."

Stephanie hesitated. "I'm not sure," she said. She'd been taught that two wrongs didn't equal a right. Also her dad had always warned her and her sisters not to stoop to the level of someone who was bothering them.

The first bell rang, and Stephanie stood up. For once she was glad lunch period was almost over.

"So what are you going to do about Jennifer?" Maura asked.

"Probably just steer clear of her," Stephanie answered. "Out of sight, out of mind."

"What happens when she's not out of sight?" Allie asked. "After all, John Muir isn't some huge school. You're bound to run into her."

"When she's around, I'll just ignore her," Stephanie said confidently. "No problem."

Stephanie wrinkled her nose as a horrible scent wafted toward her. There was something truly gross being offered at the steam tables, she realized as she and her friends neared Jennifer's end of the table.

"Thank goodness I brought my lunch today," Laura commented to Jennifer and the others.

Amber stared at something unidentifiable she had left on her plate. "It's a conspiracy," she said solemnly. "They're trying to poison us."

Just then Josh Linder walked by and stopped Stephanie. Josh and Stephanie were good friends. "Hey, Steph, nice sweater," he said, and gave her a friendly wave as he left.

"Thanks," Stephanie said. She smiled and looked around for her friends, who had taken off. She noticed that Jennifer and her friends were all watching Josh. He was, after all, very cute and one of the starters on John Muir's basketball team. When he was gone, the girls glanced back at Stephanie.

"That *is* a nice sweater," said Jennifer. She turned to Justine and giggled. "Very nice!"

Stephanie felt her face go red with humiliation. Jennifer's words didn't bother her. It was the mocking way she said them. As though *nice* were something babyish and dumb.

"I guess some people just like sweaters that are totally too big for them," Jennifer went on. "The loose, dumpy look."

This is crazy, Stephanie thought. Not only is she making me feel awful, she's making me look like a total dweeb in front of everyone at our lunch table.

"Hey, Steph." Darcy returned to the table. "We noticed you weren't with us and came back for you." She, Allie, and Maura acted concerned for Stephanie. "What's going on?" Darcy asked Stephanie while eyeing Jennifer and her crowd.

Stephanie bit her lip. She didn't want her friends to know what Jennifer had said and how it had really stung. "Oh, nothing," she replied. "Josh said he liked my sweater, so Jennifer had to comment on it."

"It looks so comfy, and it's a gorgeous blue," Maura said. "I've never seen it before. Did you just get it?"

"It's D.J.'s," Stephanie told her. "She lent it to me."

"It's great having an older sister," Maura said. "You're so lucky that D.J.'s still living at home while she's in college. My older sister went away. I miss her—and I miss borrowing her clothes."

Jennifer, who had been eavesdropping, spoke up, interrupting their conversation. "Look, I have an older sister in college, too," she said. She made it sound totally boring. "But I don't need to borrow her stuff. I mean, who needs more clothes? Actually, what's really cool," she went on, "is having a big *brother*. Then you get to hang out with him and all his cute friends.

"My brother is a senior in high school and he's captain of the varsity basketball team. I get to go to all his games. Then afterward I always go out with the guys on the team for burgers and sodas. It's totally awesome."

"Wow!" Alexa said. "That is *so* cool! Do you think I could hang out with you and your brother?"

Stephanie could feel her face turn red. She was fuming with anger. Jennifer made it sound like her brother was better than D.J., and Stephanie

11

wasn't about to let *anyone* put down D.J. She had to shut Jennifer down. Now.

"Excuse me," Stephanie said in the calmest tone she could manage. "I think it's terrific that you have such a nice brother. But my sister, D.J., is also pretty great, and—"

Jennifer yawned out loud. "If you say so." Then she turned to Justine and Alexa. "My brother is giving a party next week. He said I could invite a few of my friends. Do you two want to come?"

"She is so rude!" Allie whispered to Stephanie.

"Tell me about it!" Stephanie whispered back. "I can't believe she's so determined to one-up me that she's even turning brothers and sisters into a competition!"

"As if either of you could choose your family," Maura said.

Just then Stephanie noticed something unusual—Darcy was completely silent. Her dark eyes were focused on—and blazing at—Jennifer. Stephanie was annoyed with Jennifer. Darcy, she realized, though, was furious.

When Darcy was furious—look out! Just about anything could happen.

"For your information, Jennifer," Darcy addressed the girl in an icy tone, "Stephanie *does*

12

have a brother. And he's much, much cooler than yours."

"Darce," Stephanie whispered. "What are you talking about?"

"Oh, please. Stephanie can only *wish* she had an older brother," Jennifer scoffed. "She's got two sisters and a dog."

"Well, you're right. He's not *exactly* a brother," Darcy corrected herself. "But he's absolutely, positively *better* than a brother."

CHAPTER
2

◆ ◀ ◢ ◆

Darcy, what are you talking about? Stephanie wanted to scream. She glanced around the lunch table at the faces of all her friends. They were staring at Darcy, anticipating her next sentence.

If I say I have no idea what she's talking about, Darcy will look totally dumb, Stephanie realized. She looked at Maura and Allie. They seemed equally bewildered by what Darcy said, she noticed. They were both staring at Darcy as if she'd lost her mind.

"Okay," Jennifer said. "Somebody please explain. What kind of fabulous, better-than-a-brother person is this?"

Stephanie glared at Darcy. What was she getting her into?

"Stephanie has a close friend in Paris named Jean-Pierre. He's exactly *like* a brother to Stephanie, and he happens to be extremely cool," Darcy boasted. "And *French*."

"Yeah, sure." Jennifer sneered. "Then how come no one's ever heard of him?"

"You haven't heard of him," Darcy shot back, "because you don't know Stephanie very well. Jean-Pierre visits all the time. And they write to each other constantly." She turned to Stephanie. "Isn't that right, Steph?"

Stephanie hesitated. She didn't want to tell a completely untrue story like this, but Darcy had already started it. She couldn't make Darcy out to be a jerk by disagreeing with her now—in front of everyone.

"Uh—yeah, that's right," she said.

"So if this Jean-Pierre visits all the time, when's he coming back?" Jennifer asked.

"Next week," Darcy said. She darted a glance at Allie and went on quickly before Jennifer could ask another question. "I've met Jean-Pierre. He's wonderful. He's got short, dark hair and blue eyes. And he's"— she paused—"he's an athlete! A soccer player. Plus he's a total hunk! And all his gorgeous French friends are dying to go out with my friend here."

She slung an arm around Stephanie's shoulders. "Whenever she's there, Paris is Date City for Stephanie."

"Heh-heh," Stephanie gave a little chuckle. She glanced over at Maura and Allie. They were both scowling at Darcy. Clearly they didn't think this was a good idea, either.

But what can I do? Stephanie wondered. *I have no choice now. I have to back up Darcy's story.*

Besides, Stephanie thought, Jennifer needed a lesson to stop her from being so obnoxious. Now she would finally get it.

Everyone at the table was fascinated by Darcy's story, and Jennifer was steaming. Stephanie knew it was because Jennifer was no longer the center of attention.

Maybe now she'll see how it feels to be shut down, Stephanie thought. She decided to keep Jennifer out of the spotlight for just a bit longer.

Stephanie picked up Darcy's story. "Paris is *so* amazing," she said. "Jean-Pierre always takes me to the best shops and the hottest clubs when I'm there."

"Paris, how cool!" Amber said.

"I'd love to go shopping in Paris," Gia admitted.

"Everything's very expensive there, but—ow!" Stephanie felt a sharp pain. It was Allie. She was digging her knuckle into Stephanie's back, sending a clear message: *Stop talking now!*

Darcy picked up where Stephanie had left off. "Jean-Pierre makes sure Stephanie is getting her money's worth whenever they go shopping. No doubt about it, Jean-Pierre is totally the coolest guy you'll ever meet."

"And he's so nice," Stephanie said with a dreamy sigh. She was enjoying this wild story. Allie nudged her again, but it was too late to stop. Stephanie was already swept up in the silly fun of this fantasy. "Tell me the truth, Darce. Have you ever met anyone nicer?"

"Never," Darcy said.

Stephanie bit her lip to keep from laughing. Seeing the amazement on everyone's faces was a riot. Nothing Jennifer could *ever* say or do would top this.

"He's warm and funny and totally heroic," Darcy continued. "Do you remember the time when he saved that puppy from the fire?"

"What fire?" Justine asked, hanging on Darcy's every word now.

"He saved a puppy's life?" Gia asked. "That's so sweet!"

"Stephanie said it was in all the French papers!" Darcy went on.

Stephanie widened her eyes at Darcy, hoping Darcy would realize she was signaling her not to get too carried away. Jean-Pierre was starting to sound like a French Superman. Next Darcy'd be bragging about his X-ray vision.

"Well, enough about Jean-Pierre," Allie spoke up. She grabbed Stephanie's arm and pulled her toward the door as the second bell rang. "Steph, we'd better go."

"I don't want to be late," Maura said quickly. "I'll come with you."

Stephanie was relieved that the bell had rung. She wanted to shut down this whole ridiculous story before it went any further. It was fun, but it was getting out of hand.

Stephanie glanced at Jennifer and saw a defeated expression on her face. As silly as this Jean-Pierre story was, she realized, it had worked. Jennifer learned her lesson.

"Just a second, Stephanie." Jennifer stood up. "I don't believe you."

"Huh? Stephanie wouldn't lie," Amber said quickly.

Stephanie's heart did a quick flutter. Of course she'd been lying—although she hadn't seen it that way at the time. It seemed more like they were goofing on Jennifer.

"Darcy's right," Jennifer went on. "I guess I *don't* know you very well, Stephanie. I certainly didn't know you were such a total liar."

"I'm not a liar!" Stephanie said, stung. She glanced down the lunch table and saw doubt on her friends' faces.

If Jennifer thought she was a phony, then maybe everyone else did, too.

And if that were the case, Stephanie could kiss her entire social life good-bye.

"Okay, if you're not a liar," Jennifer said with a smile, "prove it."

Stephanie's palms began to sweat. *Prove it?* she thought. *How could I possibly do that?*

Stephanie's mind raced. "I'll bring one of Jean-Pierre's letters to school," she offered. She figured that somehow she could fake a letter from France.

"Not good enough," Jennifer told her. She glanced at Alexa and Justine. "Darcy just told us Jean-Pierre visits all the time. So why don't you just introduce us?"

"Yeah!" Amber said enthusiastically. "We'd really like to meet him."

Stephanie wavered just a second. Part of her really wanted to stop the whole story. But the rest of her knew that everyone was starting to believe Jennifer—that everyone was starting to believe that she was a liar. Her whole reputation was at stake. She couldn't back out of it now.

"I'm not sure when he'll be here. Probably sometime next week," Stephanie said. "But when he comes, I'll bring him in to meet everyone."

"Do you have a picture of him?" Laura asked. "I'd love to see him. Plus, I want to see if he's as cute as Jen's brother. How old is he?"

Stephanie shrugged. "About sixteen," she replied.

"Yeah, well, maybe I'll believe you if I see a picture of this Jean-Pierre. Bring it in Monday," Jennifer ordered. "Otherwise everyone here will know you lied about the whole thing."

"No problem," Stephanie said.

"Good," Jennifer said. "Then we can all judge how cute your French *brother* really is."

Jennifer whirled and walked away from the lunch table. Stephanie watched her go. A sick feeling filled the pit of her stomach.

On Monday she would have to show everyone a photo of a gorgeous French "brother." A boy she had never even met.

CHAPTER 3

◆ ◥ ◆ ◆

"What were you two thinking?" Allie exclaimed as she walked home with Darcy, Maura, and Stephanie that afternoon.

"We *weren't* thinking. We were just mad," Darcy said. "What's the big deal!"

"The big deal is that now Stephanie has to produce a brother or she'll look ridiculous," Maura pointed out. "Everyone will think she's a total liar. And no one will ever trust her again."

Stephanie winced. "Don't remind me."

"Don't worry, Steph," Darcy assured her. "There's always Plan B."

"Plan B?" Stephanie asked hopefully.

"Sure. You can always move to another country," Darcy joked.

"Thanks." Stephanie rolled her eyes. "That's very helpful." She turned to Allie. "For the time being, all I have to do is produce a photo. You wouldn't happen to have a photo of Jean-Pierre that I can use, would you?"

"I've never seen a picture of him," Allie admitted. "I can ask my parents, but I'm sure they would have shown it to me if there were one." She looked at Stephanie with concern. "I don't think you're going to be able to pull this off," she said. "You'll just have to admit that the whole thing was a joke."

"I'm dead," Stephanie muttered as she started up the steps of her house. "I'm completely and totally dead."

She opened the door and walked into the living room. Her jaw dropped in amazement. "Change that—I've died and gone to heaven!"

"Wow!" Allie said in a stunned voice. "What is going on here?"

The Tanner family's living room was filled with—guys! Gorgeous college-age guys! Stephanie saw guys on the sofa, on the stairs, gathered around the television. Each one was more gorgeous than the next. Stephanie stared at their rippling muscles and broad shoulders.

"This is a dream, right?" Darcy murmured. She gazed, stunned, at the crowd of hunks in front of her. Allie and Maura wore similar shocked expressions.

The thirty or so gorgeous young men seemed mostly unaware that the girls had come in. They were reading papers they held, or else they were shuffling through photographs of themselves.

Stephanie blinked hard and pinched herself. Ow! No, she hadn't died and Darcy wasn't dreaming. These guys were really there, milling around her living room, for who knew what possible reason. They seemed to be waiting for something.

"Next!" came a firm voice from behind the swinging kitchen door.

"It's D.J.," Allie whispered.

It *was* D.J., Stephanie knew.

A tall, great-looking guy with black hair, big brown eyes, and broad shoulders came out of the kitchen. Another guy, slim and blond, got up from the couch and entered the kitchen.

"Where did they all come from?" Allie asked.

"Who cares?" Darcy said with a giggle. "Oooh! I like that blond over there. The one with the surfing T-shirt—and the guy with the black hair and all the muscles—and the guy with long brown hair—"

"We get the picture, Darce," Maura said. "You like them all." She gazed around the room again. "Maybe we wandered into the wrong house," she suggested with a laugh.

"I don't think so," Stephanie joked, "but let's find out for sure. Follow me."

Stephanie headed across the living room and entered the kitchen.

D.J. and her friend, Kimmy Gibbler, sat at the kitchen table—with the blond guy. In her hand D.J. held a large color photo of him.

"So, tell me . . . uh . . ." D.J. consulted the back of the photo for his name. "Derek. Why do you want to be in the Most Attractive Men at San Francisco University calendar?" she asked. "What do you feel sets you apart from the other guys on campus?"

"I have a lot to offer the school as a competitive swimmer," he replied, "and as a reporter on the school paper. Plus, I think it would be fun to be in the calendar."

"Do you think of yourself as a hunk?" Kimmy asked.

Stephanie and her friends giggled at the question. Stephanie shook her head, smiling. That was Kimmy. Stephanie was used to Kimmy's wackiness because D.J. and Kimmy had been friends forever.

Derek blushed slightly. "No . . . uh . . . I never have . . . but some friends suggested I enter for the fun of it."

Good answer, Stephanie thought. It didn't make him sound too conceited.

Kimmy gave Derek a serious look. "If you were a flavor of ice cream," she asked, "what flavor would you be?"

"Excuse me?" Derek said as if he weren't sure he'd heard correctly.

"Never mind," D.J. told him, rolling her eyes at Kimmy. "Thanks for coming by. When we make our final decision, we'll let you know."

"What do you think my chances are?" Derek asked.

"I can't tell you until we see everyone," D.J. replied. "There are only twelve months in the year, and you can see how many guys are applying."

He nodded, then smiled. "All right. Don't forget me."

"We won't," Kimmy assured him. Derek

turned to leave the kitchen, and Kimmy blew him a kiss.

"What's all this about?" Stephanie asked as soon as Derek was out the door.

"One sec," D.J. said. She went to the kitchen door and poked her head out into the living room. "I'm sorry, guys," she said to the waiting crowd. "We have many more applicants than we expected. We've seen so many today, we just can't think straight anymore. Could you all possibly come back at the same time tomorrow?"

There was a wave of grumbling and disappointment in the living room. One by one the guys got up and headed for the front door.

"Thanks," D.J. said. "I'm sorry you had to wait."

"Why did you do that?" Kimmy asked as D.J. stepped back into the kitchen. "I'm not one bit tired. I could interview gorgeous hunks for all eternity."

"Yeah, and I'll help you if need a break," Darcy offered.

D.J. slid back into her chair. "Well, I'm tired. One guy was starting to look like the next. I've looked at so many bios and photos that I can't see straight."

Stephanie couldn't take it any longer. "Will you *please* tell me what's going on?" she asked.

"Sorry, Steph," D.J. said. "We're putting out a calendar: The Most Attractive Men at S.F.U. It's a fund-raiser for the university. Kimmy and I are the selection committee."

"Our job is to select the twelve hottest guys on campus," Kimmy explained. She giggled. "It's a tough job, but someone's got to do it."

"How did you two manage to get that sweet assignment?" Darcy asked.

Kimmy grinned and patted D.J.'s shoulder. "Because I'm best friends with the genius who came up with the idea for the calendar," she explained.

"Way to go, D.J.!" Stephanie said. "That is an awesome scheme to meet cute guys."

"That's not why I did it," D.J. said. "I just thought it would be something everyone would get a kick out of. And that it would sell really well."

"It can't miss," Maura said. She began inspecting the photos on the table. "Look at these guys!"

D.J. yawned. "It's more work than I expected."

"Hey, Steph," Maura said. "I just had an idea.

Maybe you could find a picture of your cute older brother in this pile."

"Huh?" D.J. asked. "What cute older brother?"

"You don't want to know," Stephanie assured her, but she felt a surge of hope. Stephanie picked up a handful of photos and flipped through them. The guys were all certainly cute enough to impress Jennifer and her friends. There was just one little problem.

"They're all too old," Stephanie said with a sinking heart.

"Too old for what?" D.J. demanded.

"I think they're the perfect age," Kimmy observed.

"Stephanie," D.J. said, "what are you talking about?"

Stephanie gave her sister a pleading look. "It's too complicated to explain," she said. "At least right now. I'll tell you later, okay?"

"Okay," D.J. agreed reluctantly. "Later."

Stephanie grabbed some chocolate milk, pretzels, and crackers from the kitchen. Then she and her friends headed back into the living room.

Stephanie munched thoughtfully on a pretzel. "There's got to be a way to get out of this," she said. "The guys that D.J.'s looking at are too old. And they all look like models. We need someone cute—but not someone who looks like he's just walked off the pages of *GQ* magazine!"

She looked at Allie again. "Allie, are you absolutely positive there's not a single picture of the real Jean-Pierre anywhere in your house?"

Allie sighed. "My parents have been in contact with a program director. I know he gave them a *description* of Jean-Pierre, but we haven't gotten any snapshots." Her green eyes brightened with excitement. "Hey, wait a minute! I remember my mom going through a brochure the agency sent her. I'm sure there were pictures of candidates in it!"

"That's great!" Stephanie said. "That might solve the whole problem." She finished her milk and stood up. "Let's go over to your house right now!"

"But, Steph," Darcy said. "You're supposed to be really close with this guy. And this will be a picture cut out of a brochure. How are you going to explain that?"

"I'll think of something," Stephanie told her, impatient to get to Allie's house.

"Say he was listed in *Who's Who Among French High School Students* or something, and he sent you the picture from it," Maura suggested.

"Perfect," Stephanie said. She pulled on her denim jacket. "Are you guys ready?"

"In a minute," Darcy said, taking another gulp of chocolate milk.

Allie put on her jacket. "I'm not absolutely positive my mom still has that brochure. But it's worth a shot," she said.

"At this moment it's the only thing standing between me and total humiliation," Stephanie said. "Come on. We have to at least check it out."

Stephanie yanked open the front door and started out. She shrieked as she nearly stumbled over someone sitting on the top step.

"Whoa, sorry!" A college-age guy jumped to his feet. He reached out to steady Stephanie, who was clutching the railing. "Are you okay?"

Stephanie looked up into the gray-green eyes of one the best-looking guys she'd ever seen. Her gaze traveled to his arm, where rock-hard muscles bulged from the sleeve of his black T-shirt.

"Sure, I—I'm fine," she stammered. "I guess you're here for that calendar thing. Well, I hate to tell you, but it's over for today."

He ran a hand through his short reddish hair. "Oh, I know that," he said. "And I've already had my interview."

By this time, Maura, Allie, and Darcy had come to the doorway. Stephanie looked at them, shrugged, and turned back to the guy.

"Well, then, what to you want?" she asked him.

"I was hoping D.J. would come out." He glanced down. Stephanie thought she caught a faint blush appearing on his cheeks. "I'd like to talk to her," he said.

This time Stephanie shot her friends a knowing look. This guy didn't want to talk to D.J. about the calendar. He *liked* her. He wanted to see her again!

"Wait right here," she told the guy. Then she bolted back into the house. "D.J.!" she shouted. "Someone's here to see you. He's out on the steps." She lowered her voice as she found her sister in the kitchen. "And you won't believe what he looks like!"

"Really?" D.J. asked. "Who is it?"

"I don't know," Stephanie replied. "But if I were you, I'd find out—and quick!"

She turned and headed back toward the door. "I wish I could stick around for this," she called over her shoulder. "But I have to go to Allie's."

Stephanie headed back out the door. Allie, Darcy, and Maura were waiting for her at the curb. The gorgeous guy was still sitting on the top step.

"D.J. will be right out," Stephanie told him.

She joined her friends and glanced back up. D.J. had just appeared at the doorway.

Darcy nudged Stephanie. "They're talking," she whispered. "And they're giving each other those goofy smiles."

"He likes her!" Allie added with a giggle.

D.J. must have heard them. "Will you guys please get out of here?" she shouted down.

"All right, all right," Stephanie said. She and her friends started off toward Allie's house.

"It's so cool that that guy is flirting with D.J.," Darcy said.

"I know," Stephanie agreed. "She'd be totally lucky to go out with him."

"Why?" Maura asked. "You don't know what he's like."

"Yes, I do," Stephanie insisted. "He's cool and he's cute. Just like the picture of Jean-Pierre that we're going to show Jennifer!"

CHAPTER

4

◆ ◀ ◢ ◆

"Hello!" Allie called out as they stepped into her front hall. "Anybody here?"

No one answered.

In the kitchen she found a note on the table. "My parents are food shopping," she reported. "They'll be home by supper time."

"Supper time?" Stephanie asked. She glanced at the clock on the kitchen wall. "That could be an hour or two! I can't wait that long to ask them about a picture of Jean-Pierre! I'll go crazy!"

"Why don't we see if we can find the brochure without them?" Darcy suggested.

Allie shook her head. "I can't rummage

through my mother's personal stuff," she said. "I'd get into huge trouble."

"What if we just search in the places you're allowed to go through?" Stephanie asked Allie. "We have to find it. I won't sleep tonight if we don't. I'll just be awake worrying."

"Okay," Allie said. "Let's all check the kitchen drawers first. Then we'll go through the dining room cabinets and the living room closets."

Maura pulled out a drawer filled with steak knives. "We've got to find it," she said. "You know Jennifer is dying to make Stephanie look bad on Monday. And she will if Stephanie doesn't show up with a picture of Mr. Amazing."

"I know," Allie said as she checked through the shelf filled with cookbooks. "With this horrible new personality she's adopted, she seems to think she'll become popular by trashing other people."

"You should have heard her putting down Alan Gross the other day," Maura said. "She kept making fun of his name. As if it mattered. She's really vicious."

Stephanie felt her heart begin to pound. She was not looking forward to Jennifer's being really vicious on Monday.

Darcy gazed at Stephanie sympathetically. "You really got yourself into a mess this time."

"I got *myself* into a mess?" Stephanie shrieked.

"You sure did," Darcy agreed.

"I wasn't the one who came up with this whole big story about having a brother," Stephanie reminded her. "I was only backing up your story."

Allie surveyed the kitchen. "I don't think the brochure is in the kitchen. We'd better move on to the living room."

Darcy continued the argument there. "Well, *I* wasn't the one who said I could produce a photo of the guy! That was your big idea."

"Jennifer backed me into a corner—which I wouldn't have been in if *someone* hadn't shot her mouth off about my having a brother!" Stephanie retorted.

"I was only trying to help you out," Darcy said. "I just couldn't stand there watching Jennifer be mean to you."

Stephanie sighed. "I'm sorry, Darce. I didn't mean to yell. It's just that if I can't come up with a photo of Jean-Pierre, I'm going to look like a liar in front of everyone."

"I'm sorry, too," Darcy said. She gave Stephanie a quick hug. "It's both our faults."

"I tried to warn you," Allie reminded them. She pushed up the front of an antique rolltop desk. "But you were both totally carried away by then."

"Yeah, well, you were the one who thought I should teach Jennifer a lesson," Stephanie reminded her.

Allie frowned at the contents of the desk. "I guess my mom won't mind if I go through the stuff in here," she decided. "It's right out in the living room, not really private."

Stephanie, Maura, and Darcy watched as Allie flipped through the letters, bills, pamphlets, and catalogues piled on the desk.

"Here it is!" she cried, triumphantly holding up a slim, glossy brochure. "This is what I saw my mom reading!"

"All right!" Stephanie cheered. "Let's get a look at this guy!"

She scanned the brochure. Slowly her smile faded into a quizzical expression. "Which one is he?"

"None of them," Darcy said as she read through the brochure with Stephanie. "This thing just tells about the program and has a few photographs. It's not a list of students."

"I told you I wasn't sure," Allie apologized.

"Look," Maura said. "We don't actually need a picture of Jean-Pierre. Just someone who fits the description that Darcy gave Jennifer."

"Right," Stephanie agreed. "Let's see . . ."

Stephanie flipped through the brochure frantically. She saw pictures of blond-haired boys and boys with curly hair and scrawny boys with freckles. None of them even came close to matching Darcy's description.

She turned as the front door opened. Allie's parents came in the front door carrying brown grocery bags. "Hi, girls," Mrs. Taylor called.

Allie trailed behind her parents to the kitchen. Darcy, Maura, and Stephanie were right behind her. "Mom, do you have a picture of Jean-Pierre?" Allie asked. "We can't wait to see what he looks like."

Setting down her bags, Mrs. Taylor shook her head. "They've never sent us a photo. They just gave us a description so that we could identify him at the airport."

"Oh, man," Darcy sighed, sinking into a chair.

"But that means you know what he looks like, don't you?" Stephanie asked.

"More or less," Mrs. Taylor agreed. "Let's see . . . they told us he has dark brown hair and blue eyes."

"Didn't the description also say he was studious-looking?" Mr. Taylor asked.

"Or serious-looking, I'm not sure which," his wife answered.

She put away a few groceries, then asked Allie to unpack the rest while she and Mr. Taylor brought more bags in from the car.

Slowly an image of Jean-Pierre began to form in Stephanie's mind. She saw gleaming, short, dark hair. Deep, soulful blue eyes. Just the slightest hint of a serious smile that said *I'm a sensitive person, an interesting guy to know.*

Yes, she could definitely work with that description.

Maura, who was helping put canned soups away, glanced at Stephanie. "What are you thinking?" she asked.

Stephanie tapped her fingertips on the table. "I'm thinking," she replied, "that with that description, I can just snap a picture of any cute guy with dark brown hair and blue eyes."

"That's a great idea!" Darcy said. "You're a genius."

"Hold on," Allie objected. "Remember, the real Jean-Pierre will be here next week. He'll be going to the high school, not John Muir. But what if Jennifer sees him?"

"Good point," Stephanie said. "I know. I'll take a blurry kind of picture. Or one from a distance. And the side. Maybe I can even find a guy wearing a hat."

Allie smiled. "It might work."

"Don't say *might* work," Stephanie said. "It *has* to work!"

CHAPTER
5

♦ ◂ ◾ ♦

"See any good candidates?" Stephanie asked her friends.

"Nope, no dark-haired, blue-eyed, good-looking high school guys in sight," Maura reported.

Darcy jerked Stephanie's arm and yanked her into the entrance of a Gap store. Allie and Maura scrambled in after them. "What?" Stephanie asked. "What's going on?"

Peering carefully out the door, Darcy directed their attention to a well-built, good-looking guy walking toward them with a friend. "Look at him!" she whispered. "He's exactly the way I picture Jean-Pierre!"

Allie stuck her head even farther out the doorway. "Do you think so?" she asked.

Darcy pulled hers back in. "You can't stare at him like that," she scolded.

"How else am I going to get a look?" Allie objected.

Stephanie saw that the boys had stopped at an ice-cream stand just across the way. The dark-haired boy did seem like he might be the Jean-Pierre type, but she needed to see him from a better angle.

Stephanie dug into her daypack and drew out a pocket mirror. Her heart raced as she walked out of the store and crossed over to the ice-cream stand. Could she really pull this off?

Let's just hope he doesn't notice, she thought.

Trying to act casual, Stephanie stopped a few feet from the boy. She turned her back to him and held the mirror up as if she were checking her makeup. Really she was checking out the boy over her shoulder.

He was angled away from her, which made it difficult to see him very well. Then he turned!

Eeew! No way! she thought.

She hurried back to her friends. "A definite no," she reported.

"Why? From here he looks perfect," Maura said.

Stephanie shook her head. "Three nose rings. Major turnoff."

They continued on, searching. "*There's* a possibility," Allie said. She pointed toward a guy by the food court escalator.

Stephanie turned to see a cute guy in a baseball cap. She considered him critically. He had a strong chin, very blue eyes, and a nice build. *He* was a definite possibility.

"Go take his picture," Darcy urged.

Stephanie felt suddenly nervous. "Should I just walk up to him and ask to take it?" Her friends nodded. She shook her head. "No. I can't. I would feel too funny."

"Pretend you're taking a picture of something right behind him," Maura suggested.

"Okay," Stephanie agreed with a nervous smile. She tried to appear casual as she sauntered past the boy. "What a great-looking potted palm!" she said out loud, pretending to be amazed by the palm tree behind the boy.

She got into position and framed the palm and the boy together in the viewfinder of her camera. *Perfect!* she thought.

"Hey, why are you taking a picture of that plant?" a woman asked loudly.

"Uh . . . " Stephanie said, flustered. "I . . . uh . . . I just really like potted palms. I—I have a whole collection of photographs of them at home."

"Weird," the woman said. "Very weird."

Stephanie's face flushed with embarrassment. "Well, who asked you?" she muttered as the woman walked away.

Stephanie turned back toward the boy to snap his picture.

"Oh, no!" she gasped. The boy was gone, and she'd never even had a chance to click the shutter!

She turned to see her friends laughing hysterically. "Well, now we know what's wrong with you," Darcy said. "You have a weird thing for plants."

Stephanie grinned. "All right, I guess it did sound kind of funny. But I lost the shot of that guy completely."

"Hey! Try *that* guy," Maura suggested, nodding toward a boy sitting alone, reading a book on a bench. "He looks the part."

"Absolutely," Stephanie agreed. He was very handsome, had short, dark hair, blue eyes, an

44

athletic build—and he was reading! He was exactly what both Darcy *and* Mrs. Taylor had described.

"Problem solved," she said confidently. "It really wasn't so hard. I mean, was this a good idea, or what?"

"Yes, you're a genius. We all know it," Darcy teased her. "Now go take the picture!"

"This time, though, I'm using a different approach." Stephanie nodded. "Be *right* back."

Boldly, she walked up to the boy. When she was only a few feet away, she lifted her camera and framed him in the viewfinder.

"Hey," he said. He'd raised his head and was staring directly at her.

Startled, Stephanie let the camera drop to her side. "Do . . . uh . . . do you mind if I take your picture?" she asked, not knowing what else to say.

"Why do you want to take my picture?" he asked with a friendly smile.

"For school . . . a school project," she said, which was sort of the truth.

"Sure, I'll help," he said.

He gave her a dazzling grin. "How about like this?" he asked. He held up his book and pretended to read.

"Great," Stephanie told him. "That's probably the shot I'll use. Could you give me one more, just to be safe."

After this, Stephanie thought, she and her friends could go home. She'd have the perfect picture. This *was* a brilliant plan, she congratulated herself. Sometimes she really impressed herself.

The guy stood and posed with one foot up on the chair. As Stephanie angled her camera for the perfect picture, another person walked into the field of her viewfinder. Jennifer.

Jennifer?

Stephanie swung the camera down to her side. What was Jennifer doing with *this* guy?

Jennifer looked equally surprised to see her. "Why are you photographing my brother?" she asked.

"Your . . . br-brother?" Stephanie stammered. *Oh, man!* she thought. *Of all the rotten luck!*

"It's for a school project," her brother explained.

"Really?" Jennifer let out a hoot of nasty laughter. "Could that project be called Finding Jean-Pierre?"

"No!" Stephanie insisted firmly. "The project

is for English. It's a photo journal of life at the mall.''

''Oh, right!'' Jennifer laughed.

''Don't worry,'' Stephanie said. ''I have the picture of Jean-Pierre for you.''

''I can't wait to see it,'' Jennifer scoffed.

''Monday,'' Stephanie said, and walked back to her friends.

Darcy, Allie, and Maura were standing in front of the window of a bookstore.

''Well, *that* could have gone better,'' Stephanie told them.

''No kidding,'' Allie said. ''I'm telling you, Steph, this scam is not working. I can't believe you wound up photographing Jennifer's brother!''

''Well, he *is* cute,'' Darcy said. ''Super cute.''

''Yeah, and he was really nice, too,'' Stephanie said glumly. ''Let's go home. Now Jennifer knows we were at the mall taking pictures. She'll never believe any photo with a mall background.''

''That's true,'' Maura agreed. ''But where are we going to find a picture of a phony Jean-Pierre now?''

''I wish I knew,'' Stephanie said. ''I don't even want to think about Monday. I'm going to look like a complete liar in front of everyone at the lunch table!''

*   *   *

That evening Stephanie trudged into her house feeling thoroughly defeated. She threw herself onto the living room couch. *If only there were a way I could mail-order a brother,* she thought.

She'd never really wanted a brother. The thought had never even occurred to her. But, boy, would one come in handy now.

The delicious smell of dinner cooking wafted in from the kitchen. Stephanie's stomach gave a loud growl. *I'm starving,* she realized. She hopped off the couch and went into the kitchen, where the rest of her family was already seated.

"I was just about to call you," her father, Danny, greeted her from the stove. "Have a seat and prepare yourself for my Hungarian beef goulash—made a brand-new way."

Stephanie smiled at her dad. He was an excellent cook, and his dinners were usually pretty great.

With nine people in the house, Stephanie's family sometimes ate in shifts. They could get too busy with their various activities to get together for dinner every night. But looking around the table, Stephanie saw that everyone was present and accounted for tonight.

She slipped into the empty seat between her

uncle Jesse and aunt Becky. They lived in their own apartment—on the top floor of Stephanie's house—with their twin four-year-olds, Nicky and Alex.

Uncle Jesse was her mother's brother. He moved in—to help her father take care of Stephanie and her sisters—when she was very young, just after her mother had died. Then he married Becky, who co-hosted with Danny a TV show called *Good Morning, San Francisco*.

"Did you hear D.J.'s big news?" Aunt Becky asked Stephanie.

"Actually, Stephanie was the first person in this family to meet Gary," D.J. told Aunt Becky.

"Gary?" Stephanie asked.

"The totally cute guy who was waiting for me on the steps," D.J. explained. "He asked me out."

"That's great, D.J.! How cute is he?" nine-year-old Michelle asked.

"Michelle! Since when do you care if a guy is cute?" Danny asked in surprise. He brought the steaming goulash to the table.

Michelle blushed. "Well, I *don't* care. But, I mean, I know what *cute* is. Everybody knows what cute is."

Joey, Stephanie's dad's friend who also lived

with them, began talking in a comical German accent. "Hey, cute is cute. You don't have to be a *zientifig* genius like me to know *dat*." He turned to Michelle. "Isn't *dat* right, my *leedle* munchkin?"

Michelle giggled and seemed grateful that Joey had turned this into a joke. *"Dat's* right," she replied, trying to imitate Joey's accent. "Cute is cute."

"So, what happened with Mr. Cute . . . I mean Gary?" Stephanie asked. She leaned toward D.J., eager to hear every detail.

D.J. told her how Gary asked her to go to the movies with him that weekend.

"That's great!" Stephanie said. "I could tell he liked you."

"I came in as he was leaving," Becky said. "What a doll!"

"Hey," Uncle Jesse grumbled, scowling at her.

"No one could be as completely adorable as you, dear." She patted his hand, and Uncle Jesse grinned.

"But," she added, turning back to the girls, "I can certainly see why D.J. is on cloud nine over Gary. What a dreamboat!"

"I agree one hundred percent," Stephanie said. "Totally cute!"

"You're so lucky, D.J.," Michelle added excitedly.

"Wait a minute," Danny said as he served himself some egg noodles. "Why is everyone assuming D.J. is the lucky one? First of all, I think this guy's pretty lucky to be dating D.J. And second, none of you knows anything about him. It's too early to tell if D.J. is lucky or *un*lucky here."

"Yeah," Uncle Jesse agreed. "What if he's a real dolt? A complete dummy."

"Oh, I talked to him. He's very interesting, not a dolt at all," D.J. insisted.

"Yeah? Tell me the most interesting thing he said," Uncle Jesse challenged.

D.J. thought a moment. "I can't remember, but his eyes are this cool gray-green color. They shift from gray to green, depending on how you look at them."

"That proves my point!" Danny said, slapping the table. "You can't remember one thing he said."

"Who cares what he said?" Stephanie giggled. "Why does he have to say anything?"

"That's right," Aunt Becky agreed with a mischievous gleam in her eye. "He's probably an excellent listener, a rare and attractive trait in a man."

"Besides, I'd be too busy looking at him to

hear anything he had to say," Stephanie said, smiling.

"The females in this house have lost their minds," Danny decided.

"*Ya*," Joey agreed, still speaking like a German doctor. "*Dey* suffer from acute cute-itis."

"You know," Danny said, "I can remember Becky, D.J., and Stephanie all saying that guys shouldn't judge girls by their looks, that beauty is only skin deep, and it's what inside that counts."

"It *is* what's inside that counts," Aunt Becky agreed. "But there's nothing wrong with dating a nice guy who also happens to be the cutest guy in San Francisco." She gave D.J. a wink. "It's nice to be around attractive people."

"That reminds me," D.J. said to Stephanie. "A new family just moved in across the street. They have a really cute son. He looks like he's around your age. You should go over and introduce yourself to him."

"They're still moving in," Michelle added. "He might be outside now. I saw him carrying boxes in right before dinner."

Stephanie pushed back her chair. There hadn't been a new neighbor on the block in a while. And, cute or not, a neighbor her own age was definitely interesting.

"Can I go take a look, Dad?" she asked. "I'll be right back."

"I don't believe this!" her father said.

"Oh, let her go," Aunt Becky said. "She just wants to take a peek."

"Just a peek," Danny said, giving in reluctantly. "Then I want you back at the dinner table with your family."

"Thanks." Stephanie bolted from the kitchen into the living room. She peered out the front windows. Sure enough, a man, a woman, and a boy about her age were unloading boxes from a large van.

Wow! Stephanie thought. *I can't believe I didn't notice that big van before. I must have been too caught up in this whole Jean-Pierre situation.*

Stephanie squinted her eyes to look more closely at the teenage boy. He *had* to be the son D.J. was talking about. She leaned so close to the glass that her nose touched it. The sun was setting and it wasn't so easy to tell—but she thought he had dark hair. He seemed to be very good-looking, too, with a strong, athletic build.

Dark hair.

Good-looking.

Could his eyes possibly be blue? Stephanie wondered.

Could he possibly make a good Jean-Pierre?

CHAPTER

6

◆ ◀ ◗ ◆

"Did you see him?" D.J. asked when Stephanie returned to the kitchen.

She nodded and began eating her goulash as quickly as possible. She knew her father would insist she finish eating before going across the street. She had to hurry, though. She wanted to get a better look at this guy, and she wanted to get outside before they finished unloading the van.

"You don't seem too impressed," Aunt Becky observed.

"Of course not. What's a cute boy compared to my goulash?" Danny kidded.

Stephanie swallowed hard and turned to her father. "Can I be excused?"

"Dishes," he reminded her.

"Not my night," she replied.

"Okay, you can go."

Stephanie jumped up. She darted into the living room for her camera, which she'd left on the couch. Maybe her new neighbor wouldn't make a good Jean-Pierre, but then again, maybe he would. She wanted to be prepared.

She hurried outside. With a quick glance at the traffic, she raced across the street. She slowed her pace as she neared the house, though. It wouldn't be good to show up looking like a frantic lunatic.

Trying to appear casual, Stephanie approached the front gate. The boy had gone in. Should she ring the bell? She could simply say she wanted to welcome them to the neighborhood. But what if his parents answered? They might thank her and then shut the door.

Stephanie walked slowly to the end of the block, then turned and began to walk back. If he came out now, it would look as if she were just getting home. *How can I get him to come outside?* she wondered. *How can I get him to let me take his picture?*

A figure stepped out of the door. Stephanie

quickened her pace again, not wanting to miss him this time.

The boy was taking a large duffel bag from the van when she met up with him. "Hi," she said. "Welcome to our neighborhood!"

He looked at her blankly.

A wave of panic hit her. How lame! *Welcome to our neighborhood!* Who did she think she was, Mister Rogers?

The boy smiled. Stephanie felt all her panic wash away. "Hi, I'm Matt. Thanks for the welcome."

"I'm Stephanie," she introduced herself. She stared into his eyes. It was hard to tell in the dusk light. Were they gray or blue?

"So where do you live?" he asked.

"Oh," she said. "Right over there." She pointed to her house. "We're practically neighbors. Where are you from?"

"Montreal, Canada," he replied. "My dad's business transferred him here."

Stephanie took a step closer. Yes! His eyes were definitely blue! She felt almost giddy with relief.

Then she remembered—conversation. She had to make an effort to *talk* to the boy. "Your dad's being transferred must be hard for you," she said. "Are you in high school?"

He nodded. "A junior. Yeah, I don't know a single person around here."

"The kids at the high school are nice," she assured him. "I'm in ninth grade at the middle school."

"I'll be going to Emberly Hall," he said. "I wish I were going to the local school."

Stephanie had to stop herself from doing cartwheels. Emberly Hall was an all-boys prep school. Not only did Matt look like the Jean-Pierre Darcy had described, but he was safe! Foolproof! No one knew him. No one would ever see him in school and find out he wasn't really Jean-Pierre.

"I hear Emberly's a good school," Stephanie forced herself to say. She had to bite her tongue to keep Matt from knowing how excited she was.

"It's got a great wrestling coach," he said. "I'm hoping I'll make the varsity team. Our team in Montreal was conference champs. . . ."

Stephanie only half listened as Matt told her about wrestling. All she could really think about was asking him to let her take his picture.

A picture she could pass off as being her fabulous French brother, Jean-Pierre.

Matt was absolutely perfect for the part!

Maybe, Stephanie thought, he'd even be perfect for the part of boyfriend. After all, he was almost as cute as Gary, D.J.'s new boyfriend.

Matt suddenly changed the subject from wrestling. "Hey, can you tell me where the nearest movie theater is?" he asked.

"The nearest one is the multiplex in the mall," Stephanie said. *Maybe's he's going to ask me to a movie*, she thought. "What did you want to see?"

"It doesn't matter," he said. "I love any movie where things blow up and there's a lot of shooting. You know, heavy-duty action thrillers."

Stephanie frowned. *Okay, maybe we won't go to a movie together*, she thought. *We have completely opposite tastes!* But that was all right, Stephanie told herself. After all, she and Darcy could never agree on what to see, yet they were best friends.

"What else do you like to do?" she asked.

His eyes lit with enthusiasm, but he shook his head. "You'll think it's dumb."

"Absolutely not. Tell me," she said. What would a guy think was dumb? she wondered. Dancing? Cooking? Reading? All of those sounded pretty good to her.

"Monster trucks," Matt told her.

"Monster what?"

"Those custom-designed trucks with the gigantic wheels," he explained. "They can ride right over cars and crush them. My favorite thing is to go to monster-truck rallies with my dad. It's the greatest. Someday I'd like to customize my own truck. I have tons of models somewhere. Do you want to see them?"

Stephanie grimaced. "Er—not right now," she said quickly. "But thanks."

She glanced at him in the fading twilight. He was amazingly cute. His tastes might be a little, well . . . underdeveloped, but who cared? She could barely believe her luck. She'd found the perfect Jean-Pierre substitute right across the street!

"Listen," Stephanie said. "I need to take your picture. Would that be all right?"

"Why do you need it?"

"For school," she said. "A thing I'm doing at school."

That wasn't a lie, after all.

"Yeah, okay," he agreed. "Shoot away."

"Would you mind crossing the street so we could take the picture in front of my house?" she requested. A shot taken at her doorstep would absolutely prove that this guy was a friend of her family's. "I think the light's better over there."

Matt gazed up at the sky. "It's getting kind of dark. It's not really very good light anywhere."

"Trust me," Stephanie said. "The light's better over there."

Together, she and Matt crossed the street. He posed on her steps and she snapped his picture. He was the most perfect super brother she could imagine. He looked totally handsome, with a warm smile and broad shoulders.

Yes! Stephanie thought. This would prove she wasn't lying. Hopefully, it would also make Jennifer back off—and end this whole silly challenge!

"Thanks, Matt," Stephanie said when she'd taken several shots.

"I'd better go in," Matt said. "My parents will be wondering what happened to me. But I'll see you around, okay?"

"Sure," she said. "See you around."

With a wave, Matt crossed the street back to his house.

Stephanie found D.J. and Michelle waiting for her in the living room. She felt happier than she'd felt since Jennifer started all the trouble.

"We were watching you," Michelle reported. "Is he nice?"

"He's nice," Stephanie said.

"Cool," D.J. commented. "How come you took his photo?"

Stephanie shrugged. "He was very . . . uh . . . photogenic."

"Don't tell me you're doing a calendar, too!" Michelle said.

"Not exactly," Stephanie said. Both of her sisters were looking at her with puzzled expressions. "Let's just say he's exactly the type of guy I need."

On Monday afternoon Stephanie sat down at the lunch table and waited for Jennifer to arrive. The snapshot of Matt was in her notebook. Stephanie had it developed at a one-hour developing place. Now she had nothing to worry about. She decided to play it totally cool and make Jennifer squirm.

Jennifer appeared a few moments later and sat down between Justine and Alexa.

"All right, Stephanie," Jennifer said. "Let's see what you came up with."

Stephanie waited calmly while Gia, Laura, Amber, and Maura took their seats. Allie and

Darcy hadn't shown up yet, but she could show them the photograph later.

"You don't have a photograph, do you?" Jennifer taunted.

"I never said that," Stephanie said. She pulled the snapshot from her notebook. "I found this one," she said in a casual tone. "It was taken in front of my house the last time J.P. was here." She'd decided it made them sound even closer if she had a nickname for her wonderful *brother*.

"J.P.?" Jennifer asked as she reached for the picture. "I thought his name was Jean-Pierre."

"J.P. . . . Jean-Pierre. Duh? It's too long a name, so the people closest to him call him J.P.," Stephanie explained.

Jennifer inspected the snapshot. "Hmm," she murmured. "He does look more like a J.P. than a Jean-Pierre." Looking up from the photo, she narrowed her eyes suspiciously. "This could be a picture of anyone. How do we know this guy is from Paris? I saw you taking a picture of my brother at the mall, after all."

Stephanie rolled her eyes. "*That* is obviously not the mall," she said. She took the picture from Jennifer and passed it around to the other girls at the table.

"What a hunk!" Alexa said.

"He is totally cute!" Justine agreed.

"And he looks totally cool, too!" Gia said. "How come we don't find guys like this in the United States?"

Stephanie giggled to herself. *You can find them if you happen to live in my house,* she thought.

The photo was passed from hand to hand. Everyone who saw it agreed that J.P. was a major find. J.P. was an even bigger hit than Stephanie had hoped.

Now I've really got Jennifer! she thought. *Finally she'll leave me alone.* "Satisfied?" she asked Jennifer.

Jennifer folded her arms across her chest. "Now that I think about it, this really doesn't prove a thing," she said.

"What?" Stephanie demanded. "I just showed you—"

"I dare you to bring him to school," Jennifer said. "You told me he was coming for a visit. Why don't you bring him to the pep rally tomorrow?"

Stephanie's heart began to pound. "Uh—he won't be here tomorrow," she tried to cover.

Jennifer gave her a thin smile. "That's not what you and Darcy said earlier. Stephanie, I'm calling your bluff. Have him here tomorrow at the pep rally, or we'll all know you're a liar."

Stephanie felt as though everyone in the cafeteria were staring at her—waiting for her to respond.

Stephanie blurted out, "I'll bring him, and he'll meet *everyone!* You have my word on it."

CHAPTER
7

◆ ◂ ◢ ◆

After school that day Stephanie raced straight up to her room. She sat on her bed, grateful that Michelle was at a friend's house. She needed the room to herself. She felt sick to her stomach. She couldn't believe she'd promised to bring Jean-Pierre to the pep rally. What was she going to do?

"Visitor, Steph!" Joey called up the stairs.

A few minutes later Allie walked into her room. "Hey, Steph." Allie sat down on the end of her bed. "What's up? You don't look so good."

"You missed all the excitement," Stephanie said in a flat voice. "I took a photo of my new, gorgeous neighbor and showed it to Jennifer. I told her it was Jean-Pierre."

Allie's mouth dropped open. "Did she actually buy it?"

Stephanie nodded miserably. "Everyone did. They all agreed that he was incredibly hot."

"Even Jennifer?" Allie asked cautiously.

Stephanie put her head in her hands. "No. Jennifer dared me to bring him to the pep rally tomorrow."

"Don't tell me you agreed!"

Stephanie lifted her head. "I couldn't help it. She backed me into a corner again. It was either agree or be humiliated in front of the whole table."

To her surprise, Allie grinned. "Actually, I've got great news for you. The best. My mom just told me—Jean-Pierre arrives tonight! Isn't that great! I'm so psyched!"

"That is unbelievably excellent!" Stephanie cried. "Can I come over tonight and meet him? I have to bring him to the pep rally tomorrow. Jennifer won't believe he's real until she sees him for herself. Of course, he'll look different from the photo. But it was dark when I took the picture, so I guess it'll be all right."

"Okay, Steph," Allie said. "You can take him

to the rally, but you have to promise that afterward you'll explain to everyone that this was all a joke."

"Sure, sure," Stephanie agreed, but she was already dreaming about the pep rally. "Wait till he speaks French in front of everyone. All the girls will melt. And Jennifer James will just want to fade away."

That night it was Stephanie's turn to do the dishes after dinner. She frowned as Michelle handed her yet another stack of dishes. D.J. had eaten dinner out. But eight people were still a lot to clean up after.

Michelle poked Stephanie in the ribs as D.J. glided into the kitchen, a dreamy smile on her face. "What's gotten into her?" Michelle whispered.

Stephanie shrugged.

"He's so wonderful," D.J. said. She perched on a kitchen chair. "Everywhere we go, people stare at him. And at me! It's like being out with a movie star."

"He looks like a movie star," Stephanie agreed.

"I bet he *could* be one," Michelle said.

"He's a drama major at the university," D.J. told them. "Next month he'll play one of the lead roles in a comedy in the main playhouse on campus."

"Maybe you'll marry him and move to Hollywood and meet all the big stars," Michelle said. "Then we'll all come down to visit you and hang out with famous people."

"Whoa!" Stephanie held up her hand to stop Michelle's fantasizing. "This is only D.J.'s second time out with Gary. Slow down."

"It could happen," D.J. said. "You never know. Can't you imagine him as the leading man in a movie? I can. Easily."

Stephanie could see that her older sister was really crazy about Gary. But who wouldn't be? He was definitely as handsome as any movie star.

Stephanie glanced at the kitchen clock. Six forty-five. Allie had said Jean-Pierre would probably get to her house around seven-thirty. Stephanie finished the last of the dishes with a sigh of relief.

She hurried up to her room and took out the coolest piece of clothing she owned—a short black dress. Since Paris was the fashion capital of the world, Jean-Pierre would be used to people who dressed well.

She put on the dress, applied a little makeup,

brushed her hair, and took a quick look in her mirror. *"Très chic!"* she told herself with a giggle.

She ran back downstairs and out the front door. She stopped as she saw Matt sitting on his front step across the street. He really was awfully cute, and according to Allie's mom's description, Jean-Pierre should look similar to Matt. So not only would he be attractive, he'd be cultured and French!

She waved to Matt, and he waved back.

She had to stop herself from sprinting all the way to Allie's house. She knew that running in the short black dress would look ridiculous—and it wouldn't be easy in heels.

It seemed like hours until she finally arrived at Allie's house. Allie was sitting on the front steps. "My mom and dad should be pulling up any second," she told Stephanie.

Stephanie settled in on the steps beside her, hugging her knees excitedly. "I can't wait to see him. Do I look okay?"

"You look great," Allie assured her. "How about me?"

"You look good, too," Stephanie said. Allie was dressed in jeans and her newest shirt, a long-sleeved leopard print. Her hair was pulled into a neat, elegant twist, and she wore a little lipstick—something Allie rarely did.

Stephanie leaned back against the step. It was hard to believe that in a few minutes they'd actually meet a great-looking, intelligent, totally cool guy from France. Wait until she brought him to the pep rally! Everyone would be totally knocked out.

Allie jumped to her feet, pointing. "There's the car. It just turned the corner."

Stephanie stood beside her. This was *so* exciting. She wasn't sure why. Maybe just because France seemed so far away and she'd never met a French person before. Maybe it was because she'd thought so much about J.P. that she couldn't wait to meet him.

The car pulled up to the curb in front of the house. Stephanie bent sideways to get a better view of the person sitting in the backseat. A tall young man leaned forward and began to climb out of the car.

As he emerged, Stephanie gripped Allie's arm.

"No," she murmured as panic seized her. "No! This can't possibly be!"

CHAPTER
8

◆ ◀ ◆ ◆

"*Bonsoir*, Jean-Pierre," Allie greeted the young man as he came up the steps toward them.

"Good evening," he replied in heavily accented English.

Stephanie was too stunned to speak. How could this possibly be J.P.? He was not anything like the boy she had envisioned. Not a thing!

Sure, he had dark hair—long, stringy, dull brown hair. And he was tall, all right. *Except lanky is the word I would have used*, Stephanie thought. He was tall, skinny, and slightly hunched over. As for his blue eyes—who could tell what color they were? His eyeglasses, with their thick dark rims, made it nearly impossible to see their color.

Ugh! This was a disaster! J.P. was *not* the super brother Stephanie was expecting. Not at all!

What would Jennifer and everyone else think when she brought J.P. to school, Stephanie asked herself. The answer was obvious. They'd think J.P. was a nerd and Stephanie was a big liar. She'd be totally disgraced in front of the entire lunch table!

Jennifer would never let her forget it. She would mock Stephanie mercilessly for the rest of the year—and then on into high school.

Allie introduced her to Jean-Pierre. "Hello, nice to meet you," he said. His English was stiff but correct. Stephanie forced a smile, then followed Allie, Jean-Pierre, and the Taylors into the house.

As she stepped into the front hall, Stephanie felt her stomach twist. Tomorrow was the pep rally. What was she going to do?

Stephanie suddenly realized she'd been so wrapped up in her worries, she didn't even notice that everyone had moved into the kitchen. Part of her wanted to bolt out the door and run home so she could hide in her bedroom and never come out. But another part of her couldn't do that. She had to go in and be polite to J.P. After all, *he* certainly wasn't to blame for this mess.

She took a deep breath to compose herself. Then she headed for the kitchen. She found Mr. and Mrs. Taylor, Allie, and J.P. seated at the table, laughing.

"Jean-Pierre just told us the funniest story about his flight here." Allie filled her in. "Some girls on the plane thought he was the lead singer from a Dutch rock group and kept sending him love notes."

"Yeah." J.P. laughed. "A girl, she asked me for the napkin I wiped my mouth on. I said, 'Sure, of course. Take it.'"

"You let her think you were the rock star?" Stephanie asked.

J.P. shrugged and smiled. "She didn't ask if I were he. She only asked for the napkin. I figured, if she wants my dirty napkin . . ."

Stephanie laughed. It *was* funny.

Mrs. Taylor patted his shoulder. "Oh, what was the harm? You made her a happy girl and she has a great story to tell her friends."

"I know. When I gave her the napkin, she kissed my cheek, then ran down the aisle, screaming all the way to her seat." Jean-Pierre reached for the napkin holder and pretended to stash it in his shirt. "I think I want to always keep napkins with me if that is the reaction I get handing them to pretty girls."

Smiling, Stephanie pulled up a chair and sat down. J.P. seemed like a nice guy. "J.P.," she asked, "have you have ever been in America before?"

"This is my first time," Jean-Pierre answered her. He gave her a puzzled look. "What is *J.P.?*"

Stephanie felt herself blush with embarrassment. She'd been thinking of him as J.P. for so long, it seemed natural to call him that.

"Stephanie has nicknamed you J.P.," Allie explained.

"J.P.," he repeated. "I like it. It is much more American. And I've always wanted a nickname." He grinned. "Well . . . I did have one once. My grandmother used to call me Chou-Chou. In English that means cabbage-cabbage. So, as you can imagine, I was not wild about it."

Stephanie found herself laughing. J.P. was funny and nice. Also she loved the way his voice sounded. So lively, and with that great French accent.

Still, there was no way she could bring him to

the pep rally. Jennifer was expecting drop-dead cute, and J.P. was anything but that.

J.P. told more funny stories about life in Paris. Finally Stephanie realized it was getting late. She stood up and said good night. "I'll walk you to the door," Allie offered.

Just as Stephanie was about to leave, Allie grabbed her arm. "Oh, Steph! You almost forgot to invite J.P. to the pep rally," she remembered.

Stephanie checked over Allie's shoulder to make sure J.P. wasn't nearby. "I can't take him," she whispered. "He's not at all like Darcy and I described. He doesn't look a thing like Matt's picture, either."

"But he's really nice," Allie whispered in reply.

"Jennifer won't care if he's nice," she replied, keeping her voice low. "Nice is not what this is about. Jennifer is expecting *perfect*—ultimate cool."

"What are you going to do?" Allie asked quietly.

"I have no clue," Stephanie admitted. "Maybe I could stay home from school tomorrow—or for the rest of the week. Maybe a month if I can figure out how to fake mononucleosis."

"Don't you think you're being overly dramatic?" Allie asked.

"No. Actually, I don't." Stephanie sighed miserably. "I'd better go. See you tomorrow—doomsday."

It had become slightly cooler out. Stephanie folded her arms and quickened her pace to warm herself. All the way home she anguished over the problem before her. What would happen tomorrow? No matter what she did—bring J.P. or not bring J.P.—she faced utter humiliation.

By the time she reached her front steps, she was totally caught up in figuring out a solution to the problem.

"Hey!" a loud voice shouted.

"Oh, my gosh!" she gasped. She jumped back and covered her pounding heart with her hand.

It was Matt. Standing right in front of her. She must not have heard him approaching.

"You scared me to death!" she panted.

"Sorry," he apologized with a smile. "I just wanted to ask you something. There's this movie at the mall. It's called *Blow It High.* Do you want to see it with me?"

"I've never heard of it," Stephanie said. "Who's in it?"

"I can't remember his name," Matt said. "But

you might know him. He's a big star in the AWF."

"What's that?" she asked.

"You don't know?" he asked. "Hello? Earth to Stephanie. You've never heard of the American Wrestling Federation?" Stephanie didn't respond. She was too busy noticing again how totally cute Matt was.

"So, want to go?" Matt asked. "We can just make the nine o'clock show. This is the last night it's playing."

It might be fun to go to the movies with Matt. But Stephanie remembered that she hadn't done her homework. Besides, her father wouldn't let her to stay out that late on a school night. She decided not to mention that part—too embarrassing. "I can't," she said. "Homework."

"Bummer," Matt said, sounding genuinely disappointed.

He's even cute when he frowns, Stephanie thought. Why can't J.P. look like that? Jennifer was expecting the perfect brother. And J.P. was definitely not it.

Wait a minute! Stephanie stared at Matt. *So what if J.P. didn't look like Matt? No one had ever met J.P. She'd just bring Matt to the pep rally and tell everyone he was J.P.*

"Hey," Stephanie said. "Would you like to come with me to a pep rally at my school tomorrow?"

He smiled broadly. "Yeah, cool."

It would be risky, she realized. So much could go wrong. But she was desperate.

She arranged to meet him right in front of school at dismissal. "Great, I'll see you then," she said with a wave as she headed up the front steps of her house.

"Steph, you are brilliant," she told herself. This will work.

It *has* to work.

CHAPTER
9

♦ ◄ ♦ ♦

"I think it's a horrible idea!" Allie wailed. Stephanie called her that evening to tell her the plan.

"How can you say that?" Stephanie argued. "Having Matt pose as J.P. solves everything."

"It can't possibly work," Allie objected. "First of all, Jennifer will expect him to have a French accent."

"I'll say his English is beyond excellent," Stephanie said.

"But I wanted to bring J.P., the *real* J.P., to the pep rally," Allie said.

"Do you *have* to?" Stephanie asked.

"Yes," Allie insisted firmly. "I don't think it's fair that I can't show J.P. around just because you and Darcy have concocted this stupid, complicated lie."

"Okay," Stephanie said, giving in, "but it's going to seem a little strange that J.P. has a French accent and Matt doesn't. Can you try to keep him out of the way? Oh, and don't tell anyone his name."

"How am I supposed to do that?" Allie asked.

"I don't know!" Stephanie said, her voice rising. Why was Allie being such a pain about this? Didn't she understand how important this was? "You'll think of something," she said. "Allie, I'm sorry I got you into this, but you're my best friend. You have to help me. Please!"

Allie was quiet on the other end. Finally she said, "All right. We'll think of something."

Stephanie breathed a sigh of relief. "Thanks, Allie."

"Don't worry," Allie said. "Everything will be cool."

Stephanie hung up the phone and sighed. She hoped Allie was right.

The next day, moments after the final bell rang, Allie and Stephanie ran outside to the front of the school.

Jean-Pierre arrived first, riding Allie's bike. He

slowed the bike to a halt. *"Bonjour!"* he called out.

Stephanie cringed. She hoped he wouldn't be bonjouring everyone he met.

Jean-Pierre locked his bike in the rack by the door and joined them. "Hi, J.P.," Stephanie said as the three of them went inside. She turned to Allie. "Have you told J.P. about the pep rally tradition yet?" she asked in a cheerful voice.

Allie turned to Jean-Pierre. "Um . . . we have a pep rally to kick off the season and support our team, the Raccoons."

"No, not that tradition," Stephanie said. "I mean the tradition where you watch your first pep rally from beneath the bleachers."

Allie folded her arms. "J.P. wouldn't enjoy that."

"No problem," J.P. said agreeably. "I want to do all the American things the American way."

"I don't think you want to do this," Allie told him.

Stephanie widened her eyes meaningfully at Allie. Her expression said *Just do it, please!*

"Oh, fine," Allie muttered.

Thank you, Stephanie mouthed. She watched as Allie led J.P. back outside and toward the playing field.

Just in time, she realized. Here comes Jennifer.

"Hi, Stephanie," Jennifer droned. "Looks like you're all alone. You didn't *forget* to bring this fabulous French brother of yours—did you?"

"No," she started to say. "I—"

Stephanie turned—and saw Matt in the doorway to the lobby. He looked great, dressed in jeans and a sweatshirt, with the sleeves pushed up near his elbows.

"*There's* J.P. now," Stephanie announced triumphantly.

Jennifer acted stunned. Even she would have to admit that *this* J.P. was pretty awesome.

"Hi," Stephanie called out to Matt. His face lit into a smile as he spotted her. Stephanie glanced at Jennifer's shocked expression She was thoroughly enjoying this. Every second of it.

Matt crossed the lobby to them. Jennifer tossed back her hair and smiled a flirty smile. "*Bonjour, Monsieur J.P.,*" she crooned. "*Comment allez-vous?*"

Stephanie stood frozen as Jennifer continued speaking to Matt in what sounded like fluent French.

I'm dead! Stephanie thought. In a second Jennifer will know that Matt doesn't speak French. And that he's not Jean-Pierre!

CHAPTER
10

◆ ◀ ◗ ◆

Jennifer gazed up at Matt, waiting for his reply.

Stephanie wished she could disappear.

This was it—the moment she'd tried so desperately to avoid. The moment when she would look like a complete liar and a total fraud.

Matt opened his mouth—and out came fluent, rapid, *beautiful* French!

Stephanie was so astonished, she gasped out loud.

Matt glanced at her and smiled. "Sorry, Steph, I don't mean to be rude," he said. "I'll fill you in later." Then he turned back to Jennifer and continued the conversation in French. Together they went outside and started walking toward the back of the school, where the sound of the school band told them that the pep rally had begun.

Stephanie trailed Jennifer and Matt, working hard to keep her jaw from dropping in amazement. This is practically a miracle, she thought. What were the chances that Matt spoke French like a native French person? Who would ever suspect that a guy who lived to go to monster-truck rallies would be able to speak a foreign language—and so well!

They reached the bleachers, and Jennifer spotted a group of her friends. "Oh, let me bring them over to meet you, J.P.!" she said. She was so excited, she forgot to speak French.

"Oh, you speak English!" Matt said. "I thought you spoke only French."

Jennifer giggled. "I thought *you* spoke only French. Wow! Your English is perfect. No accent at all."

Just like I told you! Stephanie thought with a grin.

"Thanks," Matt replied, not seeming at all confused by any of this.

"I'll be right back," Jennifer told him. "Don't go *anywhere*."

As Jennifer ran off to get her friends, Matt

turned to Stephanie. "I guess you told her I was French Canadian," he concluded. "I forgot I told you that."

"Uh . . . yeah . . . you mentioned it," Stephanie stumbled over her words. So that explained why Matt was bilingual. He was from the French-speaking part of Canada. What an incredibly lucky break!

"One thing I didn't understand," Matt said with a puzzled expression. "Why did she call me J.P.?"

"Oh . . . it's just . . . it's really silly," she said.

"Come on. Tell me," Matt insisted.

Think! Stephanie urged herself. "It's . . . it's . . . a nickname," she said at last. "I told Jennifer I had a nickname for you, and it was J.P."

"Why J.P.? What does J.P. stand for?" he asked.

"It stands for . . . it stands for . . . " Stephanie came out with the first thought that leapt into her mind. "It stands for Just Perfect."

"Wow!" His eyes glowed appreciatively at her. "Thanks!" he said, sounding pleasantly surprised.

Whew! Stephanie thought. Crisis averted!

Jennifer returned with five of the girls from the lunch table. "Everyone, meet J.P.," she introduced him grandly. He smiled at them and waved. All five girls smiled back at him adoringly.

Stephanie was amazed at how quickly the rivalry between Jennifer and herself had been set aside. Stephanie was glad. Even if she did win their little argument, she'd never really wanted to make Jennifer feel bad. And Jennifer sure didn't seem to feel bad. Matt seemed to have won her over completely.

"J.P., I have a million questions about Paris," Jennifer said.

Stephanie froze. Paris! she thought. Oh, no! How would Matt know anything about Paris? He's Canadian!

Stephanie held her breath and again waited for disaster to strike.

"Paris is okay," Matt said. "You know the main river, the Seine, you always have to walk across it to get from one side of the city to the other. It sort of gets on your nerves after a while. I mean, back and forth, back and forth. Every ten minutes you're going over that same stupid river. You get sick of it."

Stephanie blinked hard. Was she dreaming? If so, what a great dream! She'd been saved. Again!

"So, you're saying the Seine is an *annoying* river?" Justine Murphy asked. She frowned.

"Yeah, I would say so," Matt agreed as they watched the cheerleaders run onto the field. "I'm sure glad there's no river right in the middle of San Francisco."

Stephanie had never heard a river described as *annoying*. Especially not one as famous as the Seine. Paris was a world capital, and it was supposed to be extremely romantic. Didn't Matt have anything more interesting to say about it? *Maybe I ought to stop him from talking before someone figures out that he's not the most intelligent guy in the world*, she thought.

"Hey, let's watch the pep rally," Stephanie suggested, standing beside the bleachers.

"No, we'd rather listen to J.P.," Jennifer insisted.

"Okay, but let's at least sit down," Matt said. Stephanie found herself being jostled aside as Jennifer and her pals vied for seats close to Matt.

For a while she listened as he spoke about Paris and wondered how he knew so much. Eventually he began talking about a car show that had come to the city, and she lost interest. The other girls didn't seem to mind. They continued to listen with total attention to his every word.

Bored, Stephanie suddenly remembered Allie and J.P. She spotted them, two figures sitting on the opposite side of the field under the bleachers. They were both laughing hard. They looked like they were having a wonderful time.

In fact, they looked like they were having a much better time than she was.

"And then"—Stephanie heard Matt say— "came the best day of all. The day the live wrestling show came to Paris!"

Stephanie thought she had never been at a pep rally that lasted so long. She had never known John Muir had so many cheers—or that they all went on forever!

This is endless, she told herself as the cheerleaders ran out one more time.

Finally, though, the pep rally ended. Stephanie let out a sigh of relief. The whole stupid "brother" thing was over at last!

"That was fun!" Matt said as everyone began to stream out off the stands.

"Glad you liked it," Stephanie said. "Come on, we can catch the last bus home."

They were just heading off the field, when Jennifer came up to them. "Bye, J.P.," she said. "I guess I'll see you on Friday at the kickoff dance."

"I . . . uh . . . I don't know," he answered, turning toward Stephanie.

Stephanie felt herself burning with frustration. She'd finally gotten through the whole brother charade, and now Jennifer was going to force her to keep it going!

"You are going to bring J.P., aren't you?" Jennifer asked.

"I don't know if he'd enjoy something like that," Stephanie answered quickly.

This is not what I was planning on! she thought. She hadn't intended to ask Matt or any guy. She planned on going with Darcy and Allie and Maura.

Cute as Matt was, she had no romantic feelings for him—at all. Probably because she didn't find wrestling and monster trucks very romantic.

"I'd like to go to the dance," Matt said, gazing into Stephanie's eyes. "That is, if you want me to."

"Well, do you, Stephanie?" Jennifer prodded.

The eagerness in Jennifer's voice made Stephanie realize what was going on. *She* wanted to ask Matt to the dance. She was hoping Stephanie would say no so that she could ask him.

Well, there was no way that was going to happen, Stephanie decided. Then Jennifer would not
only have a perfect-looking brother, she'd also
have a perfect-looking boyfriend to lord over
Stephanie. And Stephanie was not about to do
anything that would help Jennifer act even more
sickeningly superior than she already was.

"Sure," Stephanie said to Matt. "I'd love to go
to the dance with you."

"Great," Matt said with a smile.

Jennifer's smug smile disappeared.

Stephanie turned to Matt. "We'd better hurry
if we're going to catch that bus."

"*Au revoir, J.P.,*" Jennifer said.

"Bye, Jenny, nice to meet you," Matt replied.

"Jenny?" Stephanie questioned as they walked
toward the school parking lot to catch the late
bus. "No one ever calls her that."

He shrugged. "She told *me* to call her that."

Stephanie stopped before reaching the parking
lot. She saw Allie and J.P. standing a few feet
away.

"Are you taking the bus?" she called to Allie.

"No, J.P. is riding me home on the bike," Allie
called back. She was smiling and so was J.P.
Stephanie felt an odd surge of irritation. Seeing
Allie and J.P. so happy bothered her.

"He's J.P., too?" Matt asked.

"Yes, but *he's* not perfect," Stephanie grumbled, not quite understanding why she felt so annoyed. "He's called J.P. because his name is Jean-Pierre."

"Oh," Matt said. "Funny to have two J.P.'s."

"Yeah, it is," Stephanie agreed. "Come on."

On the bus ride home, Matt told Stephanie all about *Blow It High*, the movie he went to see with his dad after Stephanie had turned him down.

"So first they blew up a bank with dynamite," Matt explained. "And then they used this real basic pipe bomb to flatten a car factory. And then the bad guy got a hold of these super high-tech rockets . . ."

Stephanie tuned it all out. It was either that or scream. Matt was a nice guy, but his taste in entertainment drove her crazy.

Luckily, just when she couldn't take another second of *Blow It High*, the bus pulled over at their stop.

"Well, good-bye," Stephanie said as they got off the bus.

"See you tomorrow," Matt said.

Stephanie didn't want to encourage him to say

any more. She waved and hurried up the steps to her front door.

After she opened the door and went inside, she collapsed on the living room couch. The pep rally was over, and Jennifer still thought she had a super brother named J.P. Now, if she could just keep this up for the dance. . . .

"I agree with you completely." D.J.'s voice floated over to her. Stephanie sat up and noticed that D.J. was lying on her back on the living room rug, holding her cordless phone. She was smiling at the ceiling.

D.J. spoke into the phone. "That makes total sense. Of course I understand. You've got a rehearsal, so you have to go. Bye, honey. Me, too. Bye."

"Honey?" Stephanie asked when D.J. was done with her call.

Her sister smiled again. "That was Gary," she said. "Things are going great with him. He's so sweet."

"Wow! You're really into this guy," Stephanie observed.

"He always knows exactly what to say," D.J. told her. "Like this evening I was feeling a little insecure because . . . well . . . you should see how the women on campus throw themselves at him. But he always makes me feel so special. He told me I had brains *and* looks, and he doesn't often find that combination."

Stephanie smiled. "You've got it bad! But I can't blame you. He sounds pretty great."

"Tell me about it!" D.J. said with a sigh. She sat up and grinned at Stephanie. "Speaking of great, that Matt from across the street is pretty good-looking, too. Has he asked you out—or have you asked him?"

"Just as friends," Stephanie replied. "I don't think he's my type."

"What do you mean?" D.J. asked. "You don't like gorgeous guys?"

"Sure, but . . . I don't know," Stephanie said. Somehow Matt no longer seemed as amazingly gorgeous to her as he had at first. She wondered why.

D.J. stood up. "Kimmy and I picked the twelve most handsome guys for our calendar today. Want to see?"

"Definitely," Stephanie said. She followed D.J. into the kitchen. The twelve photos were stacked neatly on the kitchen table. D.J. handed them to her and Stephanie flipped through them. "Good work," she said, admiring each knockout-gorgeous guy. "Everyone will want to buy this. You'll make a fortune."

"I hope so," D.J. said, gazing over Stephanie's shoulder at the photos.

Stephanie handed the pictures back to her. "Hey, how come Gary isn't in the calendar? He's as awesome looking as any of these guys."

"I know," D.J. agreed with a dreamy sigh. "But I couldn't include him now that we're dating," she explained. "Everyone would say I played favorites if I put my own boyfriend in the calendar."

"You have a point," Stephanie said.

"I also have a report to finish," D.J. told her. "I'd better get to it." She took her photos and went up to her room.

Stephanie went to the phone and punched in Allie's number.

"*Allo*," J.P. answered.

"Hi," Stephanie replied, a smile unexpectedly spreading across her face. "It's Stephanie. How did you like the pep rally?"

"It was very . . . how do you say? . . . wacky."

"Wacky?" Stephanie laughed. "What do you mean?"

"That big raccoon was very strange. Don't you agree?"

Stephanie had a feeling that Jean-Pierre had never seen a team mascot before. "I suppose he is a bit bizarre," she agreed.

"And those jumping girls? What do you call them?"

"The cheerleaders?" Stephanie suggested.

"Yes, that is it. They are a bit crazed with enthusiasm, no?"

Stephanie laughed. It was funny to see a normal old pep rally through J.P.'s eyes. "Yes," she said, "I suppose you could see it that way."

"Of course, no one is more crazed than European soccer fans. They fight with each other all the time. So, perhaps we should get a big raccoon and cheer girls and things would be happier." He laughed. "See? I have learned something from my stay in America already. Let me write it down. 'Get big raccoons.'"

J.P. is so much fun to talk to, Stephanie thought.

"Is that for me?" she heard Allie ask.

"No, it is not," J.P. responded.

"Who is it?" Allie demanded.

"It's Stephanie," J.P. said. "She called to speak to me."

"She did not." Allie giggled. "She wants to speak to me!"

Stephanie grinned as she listened to J.P. teasing Allie. Somehow she liked the idea of his thinking that she'd called to talk to him.

"I will give you the phone," she heard J.P. say to Allie. But Allie didn't come on the line right away. Instead, Stephanie heard breathless laughter and shouts of "Come on!" and "Give it to me!" She frowned. They sounded like they were having so much fun.

"I'm sorry," J.P. joked. "Allie is too short to come to the phone."

"I am not!" Allie shouted. The phone clattered to the ground. Then Allie came on. "Sorry," she panted. "J.P. is always clowning around. He was holding the phone over my head. I had to jump for it. What's up?"

"What do you mean, what's up?" Stephanie snapped. The sound of her own irritable tone surprised her. She hadn't meant to sound like that.

"I mean," Allie said, "you called me. Why? Is that clearer?"

"All of a sudden I need a reason to call you?" Stephanie asked. "I can't just call you to say hello?"

"Of course you can. Hello."

"Oh, that's cute," Stephanie snapped. It was as if she couldn't control the irritation in her voice.

Something about Allie was really bugging her. She didn't know what it was.

Allie sighed. "I *thought* maybe you were calling to thank me for taking J.P. under the bleachers, so it wouldn't ruin your little hoax."

"Why should I thank you?" Stephanie asked. "It looked like you and J.P. were having a great time under there."

"So what? Is that a crime?" Allie shot back. "J.P. happens to be a lot of fun. What's the matter? Didn't you have a good time?"

"I had a great time," Stephanie replied. Her voice rose to a shrill pitch. "It was wonderful! Everyone adored Matt. He was a huge hit. I think Jennifer even has a crush on him." Stephanie realized she was shouting and lowered her voice. "So, it went very well."

"Good," Allie said. "Is that what you called to tell me?"

"Yes," Stephanie said. "Bye."

"Bye."

Stephanie stood with the phone receiver in her hand. Why had she spoken to Allie so rudely? Come to think of it, she'd been finding Allie annoying ever since J.P. arrived.

Slowly, she hung up. A disturbing thought came to her. Why wasn't she happy that Allie and J.P. were having so much fun together? Could she possibly be . . . jealous?

"No," she said to herself. "No way."

It simply didn't make sense. She was the one hanging out with gorgeous Matt. Allie was stuck with goofy J.P.

If anyone was jealous, it should be Allie.

Shouldn't it?

CHAPTER
11

♦ ◄ ♦ ♦

Stephanie walked into the cafeteria the next day to find Darcy at their usual table. Maura was sitting at a table by herself, scrawling in a notebook. Stephanie knew that Maura did this sometimes. Maura was a poet, and when she felt inspired, she'd go off by herself to write. But it was strange that there was no sign of Allie or the others.

"Is Allie avoiding me?" Stephanie asked Darcy.

"I don't think so. She lost a filling in math class. I think she left school for an emergency dentist visit," Darcy explained. "Why would she avoid you?"

"We had kind of an argument on the phone

last night," Stephanie said. "Nothing major, but it was weird."

"What do you think is bothering her?" Darcy asked.

"I have no idea," Stephanie said. She'd decided her idea about being jealous was too crazy. It couldn't be that. She had no reason to be jealous of Allie. Maybe she was just feeling crabby because of this whole Jennifer situation. "I'll just talk to her," Stephanie decided. "And everything will be all right."

After school that day, Stephanie went straight to Allie's house—to apologize face-to-face.

She rang the doorbell and waited, her stomach doing flip-flops. What if Allie wouldn't listen? she wondered. What if she didn't want to make up?

J.P. opened the door. "Come in," he said. "But Allie is not here. Mrs. Taylor took to her to the mall to cheer her up after a bad tooth morning."

Stephanie let out a low moan of frustration. "I really need to talk to her," she said.

"I think they'll be home soon," J.P. said. "Are you hungry? I was just about to eat."

"That sounds good," Stephanie said, following him into the kitchen.

"Would you like a crepe?" Jean-Pierre asked. She saw that he had a bowl of batter sitting next to the stove. "I was making ones with ham and cheese."

"Sure." Stephanie looked at the stove top and frowned. One burner was on. A cast-iron skillet rested on it, bottom up. "There's just one problem," she pointed out. "Your pan is upside down."

"Oh, well, right side up, upside down—what is the difference?"

"Are you joking?" she asked.

J.P. laughed. "Yes, it is a joke. I have improvised a crepe pan by using the pan bottom. Watch." With a dramatic flourish he ladled out some batter and poured it onto the hot pan bottom. Stephanie was sure the batter would run over, but it didn't. Next, J.P. added shredded ham and cheese and let them cook.

"Pretty neat," Stephanie said.

J.P. smiled at her. "The best is yet to be."

She watched as he neatly rolled the crepe, scooped it onto a plate, and set it in front of her. "*Voilà!* There you have it," he announced as he handed her a fork. "Your crepe is served, *mademoiselle*."

The steam from the warm crepe had fogged

his glasses. "Is it foggy in here or is it me?" he joked, removing them.

"It's you," Stephanie said with a laugh. As he wiped his glasses on a kitchen towel, she saw that he had the most incredible, intensely blue eyes. Stephanie felt as if she'd had the breath knocked out of her. His eyes were really amazing, Stephanie thought.

She looked away as J.P. pushed his glasses back on his nose. She hoped he hadn't realized she was staring at him.

"So how is it?" he asked.

She bit into the warm, delicious crepe. "This is unbelievably great," she told Jean-Pierre honestly. "Awesome!"

"Thank you," he said as he began making one for himself. "There is a crepe maker on every third corner in Paris. You can get all kinds of crepes, chocolate ones, sugar ones, lunch ones like this."

"Do you miss home?" Stephanie asked.

"Not yet. I am having too much fun." He sat beside her at the table. "Besides, I am much too busy. I promised the newspaper at my school back home that I would write them an article about life in America. I have started it already."

"I write for my school paper, too," Stephanie told him excitedly. "Do you like to write?"

"I love it. I hope to become a reporter someday."

"Me, too!" Stephanie cried. "That's the sort of writing I like best—news stories. Of course, fiction is kind of fun, too. But I don't think I have enough imagination for it."

"I bet you do," J.P. disagreed. "But journalism has a whole different kind of excitement. It is a completely different thing, really."

"It seems that way to me, too," she agreed. "In reporting you're sort of a detective as well as a writer. You know, uncovering facts."

"That is exactly what I like about it," J.P. said. "I do not want to be a reporter who tells only what cars crashed and who is in jail. I want to uncover scandals and wrongdoing. Possibly about the environment."

"So do I," said Stephanie as she took her last bite of crepe. "And recently I started working on a new project. The students at John Muir, my school, are producing a TV program called *Scribe TV*. I'm producer of the show, and I'm going to write some news reports for it, too."

J.P. took out two sodas from the refrigerator. "Writing for TV could be so great," he agreed.

They went on talking about TV journalism for another hour—only it seemed like minutes. Stephanie was amazed when she glanced at the clock. "Wow," she said. "Look at the time. I guess Allie and her mother are spending lots of money at the mall." She laughed uneasily, suddenly feeling awkward for the first time. Did he mind that she'd taken up so much of his time? He didn't seem to.

"I'd better go," she said, getting up from her chair. "Please tell Allie I couldn't wait any longer."

"Yes, I will," J.P. said. "It was nice to talk to you."

"It was," she agreed. "I'd really better go."

She hurried out of the house and started home. J.P. was so great. They had so much in common. How could she have ever thought he was a geek? His long hair wasn't stringy. It was actually sort of cool. Funky. Everything about J.P. was funky. He had style—individual style. And then there were those gorgeous eyes! Even his thick-rimmed glasses didn't seem so nerdy anymore. They seemed trendy. Edgy. Intellectual.

"Whoa!" Stephanie stopped short. What was she thinking?

Could it be . . . did she *like* J.P.? Like really *like* him, as in having a crush on him?

Maybe, Stephanie admitted. All she knew for sure was that he made her laugh. And she really loved talking to him. She felt excited when he was around. Yes. It seemed to Stephanie that she had all the classic signs of having a major crush on J.P.

Stephanie stopped short as another thought occurred to her. It was a thought that made her stomach churn. She had just realized how much she liked J.P.—and she was stuck taking *Matt* to the dance Friday night.

She began walking again, thinking hard about the situation. Was there a way to take J.P. to the dance? Or did she just have to get through the dance with Matt and then try to find a way to do something else with J.P.?

Does Allie have a crush on J.P.? Stephanie wondered. It could be a huge problem if she did. *Maybe*, Stephanie thought, *I'm getting ahead of myself. Maybe the first question is, does J.P. really like me—or is he just being friendly?*

Stephanie was so deep in thought that she was surprised to see that she'd already reached the front steps of her house. Glancing up, she saw Gary standing there, about to knock on the door.

"Don't bother," she said, hurrying up to him. "I have a key. I'll let us both in." She rummaged in her backpack for her front door key. "So how are things going with D.J.?" she asked just to make conversation.

"D.J. is terrific," Gary answered. "I really like her. She's so smart. That fund-raising calendar was all her idea, you know. I wonder which month I'll be."

Stephanie found the key and put it in the lock. "You're not going to be any month," she said. "You're not in it."

"What?" he shouted.

She turned and looked at him, surprised by his outburst. *Uh-oh,* she thought. *Maybe I should have let D.J. tell him that.*

"I'm not in the calendar?" he repeated as if he couldn't believe it was true.

"It wouldn't have been fair for D.J. to play favorites," Stephanie explained. "I mean, she really *couldn't* put you in the calendar if you think about it."

"Are you sure?" he asked angrily.

Stephanie nodded. "You can't blame D.J."

Gary's eyes narrowed. "I see," he said in a cold fury. Then he turned and stormed down the steps.

"Hey," Stephanie called. "Weren't you here to see D.J.?"

"Never mind," Gary said.

"Should she call you?" Stephanie asked anxiously.

"Whatever," he grumbled, hurrying away.

Oh, no, Stephanie thought. *What have I done now?*

CHAPTER

12

♦ ◂ ◾ ♦

"Oh, it's hopeless." Stephanie sighed to herself. She stared into her closet and wondered what to wear to the dance that night. Of course, she wanted to look good. But not for her date, Matt. Allie was bringing J.P. *He* was the one she wanted to impress.

"What's hopeless?" Michelle asked. She was sitting at her desk, doing math homework.

"My clothes," she said, turning to her younger sister. "They're so . . . American."

"Is that bad?" Michelle asked.

Stephanie threw herself onto her bed. "J.P. is used to girls who wear French fashion, sophisticated dressers."

"I thought J.P. was kind of geeky," Michelle reminded her.

"I was wrong. He's not a geek at all," Stephanie got up off the bed. "Do you think D.J. would lend me something to wear?"

"I would," Michelle offered.

"Thanks," Stephanie said, "but I don't think your clothes would fit. I'd better ask D.J."

Seconds later she was rapping on D.J.'s bedroom door. "D.J., are you in there?" she called.

There was no answer, so Stephanie headed downstairs to look for her sister. "D.J.?" she called.

At that moment the front door flew open and D.J. rushed in. Tears streamed down her face.

"D.J.?" Stephanie said. "What happened?"

"I can't believe he could be so horrible!" D.J. sobbed.

Stephanie had a pretty good hunch who D.J. was talking about. But she asked anyway. "Gary?"

"Yes, Gary," D.J. answered. She sat on the couch and dabbed her wet eyes with a tissue.

Stephanie sat beside her. "Oh, D.J., I'm so sorry. It's all my fault. On Wednesday I told him he wasn't in the calendar. It just slipped out. I would have told you when I came in, but you were so busy with your report. And then I forgot to tell you yesterday, and you were gone when I got up this morning."

"It's all right," D.J. said with a sniff. "I didn't see him yesterday and was in the middle of telling him myself today. That's when it all came out. He was just using me to get into the calendar!" She dried her eyes and took a deep breath. "He thought it would help his modeling career, which would also help his acting career. Can you believe it? It all came out just now, when he broke up with me."

"What a creep!" Stephanie said. "Are you okay?"

D.J. sniffed again and wiped her eyes once more. Aunt Becky came down the stairs. "D.J., what's wrong?" she asked.

"Gorgeous Gary turned out to be a gorgeous creep," Stephanie told her. "He was dating D.J. just because he thought she'd put him in the calendar."

"That's terrible!" Aunt Becky said. She took a box of tissues from the coffee table and handed them to D.J. "You probably feel used," she told D.J. "But you have to ask yourself—will you miss Gary? Or will you miss being seen around campus with Gary?"

D.J. sniffed. "What do you mean?"

"Since Gary is one of the hottest guys at school, it made you look really cool to be seen going out with him," Aunt Becky said.

D.J. sat back hard against the couch and sighed. "You mean I was using Gary, too?"

"You were not. You wouldn't do that," Stephanie said.

"Wait a minute. Maybe Becky's right. I didn't know I was doing it—but I was," D.J. said. "I was using Gary for his good looks. Dating him was a way of getting instant status, instant popularity. I told myself I liked him, but I didn't really. He was so . . . so . . . I don't know . . ."

"Smooth?" Aunt Becky guessed.

D.J. nodded. "Definitely. A smooth, devious conniver. And a user."

"Not much of a loss," Stephanie said.

"Could be worse," D.J. agreed. She gave Stephanie a wry smile. "I guess that's what you get when you let looks be so important. Looks. And not much else." D.J. stood up and headed for the stairs.

"Speaking of looks, you just reminded me," Stephanie said. "Can I borrow something to wear to the dance tonight?"

"Sure, just pass it by me before you go," D.J. agreed.

Wow! Stephanie thought. She didn't even have to plead. "Thanks," she called after her sister.

"I'd better get upstairs and see how Jesse is doing with the twins," Aunt Becky said. "Don't worry about D.J. She's tough. She'll be okay."

"I know," Stephanie said. After Aunt Becky left, she stayed on the couch a moment, thinking about what had just happened. Why was *she* feeling so uncomfortable and uneasy? she wondered. Then it hit her.

Was she another Gary?

Was she using Matt the way Gary had used D.J.? Was she using him and his good looks to impress Jennifer and get her off her back?

No way, Stephanie told herself. It isn't the same.

Saying that to herself didn't make the guilty feeling disappear, though. In her head she heard D.J.'s words again. *He was a smooth, devious conniver. And a user.*

Didn't that pretty much also describe how she was behaving?

"It's not the same," Stephanie said out loud as she got to her feet. But if it wasn't, why wouldn't this awful feeling go away?

CHAPTER

13

◆ ◥ ◂ ◆

"Everything looks so great," Stephanie said to Matt as they walked into the dance. Her eyes swept the room. The dance committee had totally converted the gym into a fantasy land with colored lights, streamers, and Chinese paper lanterns.

"It's nice," he agreed.

Stephanie was still feeling guilt pangs about going to the dance with Matt. But she wasn't manipulating him, she told herself. She wasn't dating him the way Gary dated D.J. Asking him to the dance was just a friendly invitation. Besides, this whole charade would be over soon. Then they could just be friends without any other stuff attached.

Matt reached for her hand. *Oh, no!* Stephanie thought. *Maybe he's starting to like me!*

Stephanie slipped her hand out of Matt's and pointed across the room. "There are my friends Allie and Darcy and Maura," she said, trying to make conversation. Her face suddenly lit with a smile. "Oh, and there's J.P."

"The other J.P.," Matt recalled.

"Oh, uh, that's right. Ummm . . . Matt, don't mention to him that you're also called J.P.," she said. "He . . . uh . . . thinks it's his nickname alone, and I wouldn't want to hurt his feelings."

"Okay, I guess," Matt agreed.

"Come on, let's join them," she suggested, heading across the gym.

As Matt followed her over, Stephanie was barely aware of him at her side. Her eyes were locked on J.P. And she was hoping that J.P. couldn't guess how fast her heart was beating.

"Stephanie!" J.P. said. "You look very nice tonight."

"Thanks." She smiled, pleased with D.J.'s short, acid-green silk dress. She introduced J.P. to Matt. "Both of you speak French," she added.

The two boys seemed delighted by this and instantly launched into a rapid-fire conversation in French. Leaving them to chat, Stephanie pur-

114

posely caught Allie's eye. This wasn't a great moment to apologize to her, but it would have to do.

Allie abruptly broke their quick moment of eye contact and touched J.P. lightly on the arm. "I'm getting some soda. Want some, J.P.?" she asked.

"Sure. I'll come with you," he replied. He said a few more words to Matt in French, then walked off with Allie.

Stephanie felt that old surge of irritation at Allie. Now she understood it, though. It was jealousy, pure and simple. She pushed it from her thoughts and turned to Darcy and Maura, who had come to the dance without dates. "Allie's really mad at me, isn't she?" Stephanie asked.

Maura nodded. "We found out she has been avoiding you the past couple of days."

"She says you've been totally rude to her lately, and she's sick of it," Darcy said. "What's going on?"

"I'll explain later," Stephanie answered. She felt bad about being so horrible to Allie and hoped she'd get a chance to apologize before the dance was over.

She scanned the gym floor, wondering where Jennifer was. She wanted her to see her with

"J.P." so she could get this whole charade over. She heard the flirty voice before she saw her.

"Oh, hi, J.P. Care to dance?" Stephanie turned and saw that Jennifer was talking to Matt. She looked great in a short, simple metallic-blue dress.

"Thanks, but if you don't mind, I'd like to dance the first dance with Stephanie," Matt said.

Oh, no! Stephanie thought. Either Matt really liked her or he was just an incredibly nice and considerate guy. Either way, it didn't make her feel great about bringing him to the dance, even though she didn't like him as a boyfriend.

Jennifer curled her lips into a forced smile. "Oh, isn't that cute. Brother and sister dancing together."

Matt turned to Stephanie with a confused expression. "What is she talking about?"

Stephanie swallowed hard and clutched his arm. "I don't know. Let's dance," she said, whisking him away from Jennifer before she could say anything else.

Matt slipped one arm around Stephanie's waist, and Stephanie felt her heart sink. Just what she didn't need—a slow, romantic dance with Matt!

"Why did she think we were brother and sister?'' Matt asked as he began swaying to the music.

''Oh, who knows? Jennifer's just mad because you turned her down,'' Stephanie bluffed. ''She's a little crazy.''

''She seems nice to me,'' he said.

Stephanie didn't respond to that. She was too distracted by Matt. He kept trying to draw her close, to get her to rest her chin on his shoulder.

Stephanie gazed around the room. She waved to Darcy and Maura. She stumbled and pulled back. She adjusted the barrette in her hair. She did everything she could to avoid dancing so close.

She kept noticing J.P. She couldn't seem to help looking at him. He and Allie were dancing together on the other side of the gym.

What would it be like to dance with him? she wondered. It would be wonderful, of course. Besides being so cute, J.P. was clearly a good dancer. How could she have been so wrong about him?

The next dance was also a slow one. ''Want to keep going?'' Matt asked, sounding eager.

''No, not right now,'' Stephanie admitted.

''Okay.'' Matt took her hand. ''It's getting

crowded and loud in here," he said. "Let's go out to the hall, where we can at least talk."

She couldn't think of a good reason to say no. She nodded, and Matt led the way through the gym out to the much quieter hall beside it.

"Thanks for inviting me to this dance," he said softly, taking a step toward her.

Oh, no! Stephanie realized. *He's leaning in to kiss me!*

Without even thinking, Stephanie ducked under Matt's arm and away from him.

He whirled around to face her. "What's with you?" he asked. "If you don't like me, why did you invite me to the pep rally the other day and to the dance tonight?"

"I do like you," Stephanie said. "But not in that way. I like you as a friend, Matt."

As she spoke, she noticed that Jennifer had just walked into the hallway. Jennifer stopped short at the sight of Matt and Stephanie facing each other. "Matt?" she said, her eyes darting from Matt to Stephanie. "What do you mean, *Matt*? I thought his name was J.P.—Jean-Pierre!"

Matt cast a hard gaze at Stephanie. "I thought J.P. was supposed to mean Just Perfect."

"No, it means Jean-Pierre, Stephanie's friend

from Paris," Jennifer explained. "Isn't that who you are?"

Stephanie cringed. This was it. The moment she'd been dreading. "No, Jennifer. He's Matt. My neighbor," she admitted.

"I knew it!" Jennifer crowed triumphantly.

"I don't get this," Matt said angrily. "Did you use me to win some kind of bet or something?"

Jennifer grinned at him. "She certainly did. It wasn't a bet exactly, but she tried to pass you off as her dear friend from Paris just so she could look cool in front of everyone."

Stephanie sighed. There was no sense denying it. And it would take too long to explain why she really did have to go through with all of this.

"I didn't mean to hurt your feelings," she said to Matt.

"This is nuts," Matt said, looking away from her. "Instead of lying to me and stringing me along, why didn't you just bring in the real J.P.? At least he really is a French exchange student."

"I couldn't," Stephanie said in a small voice. "I'd already said he was a gorgeous hunk and super cool. If I'd brought in the real J.P., everyone would have laughed at me."

"Oh, really?" The voice came from behind her. Stephanie stiffened.

Without looking, she knew it was Jean-Pierre.

She wished she could just disappear! Being swallowed by a giant black hole sounded way better than being there, but that wasn't going to happen. Slowly she turned to face Jean-Pierre. Oh, no. It was as bad as Stephanie thought. From his stricken expression, she could tell he'd heard her calling him ugly and uncool.

She opened her mouth to say something to him, but her throat was dry and only a croaking sound came out.

"I really was beginning to like you, Stephanie," J.P. said coldly. "I had no idea you were so manipulative. It's good I found out in time."

"J.P., please," she managed to choke out.

"I'm leaving," he said, turning away.

"Me, too," Matt said as he headed back into the gym for his jacket. "Wait for me!" Jennifer called to Matt and started after him.

Stephanie leaned heavily against the lockers and buried her face in her hands. Her stomach ached with anxiety.

This was so horrible!

She'd made a total and complete mess of everything!

There were so many things to feel awful about. Jennifer would soon be telling the entire school what a big phony she was. No one would ever believe her again. Matt was furious with her. Allie was angry at her.

But the thing she felt worst about was hurting J.P.'s feelings.

CHAPTER
14

◆ ◀ ◾ ◆

"I say he looks like a definite December to me," Kimmy insisted to D.J.

Stephanie sighed and hung her head over her bowl of corn flakes. After the Disaster at the Dance, she felt horrible—and she'd barely slept all night.

Now D.J. and Kimmy sat at the kitchen table with photos of guys spread out in front of them. And they'd been debating about the layout all morning.

"Yes. He definitely looks like a December to me," Kimmy insisted.

"How can you say that?" D.J. argued. "Look at this sweater he's wearing—orange, black, and yellow. He belongs sometime in autumn for sure."

Oh, well, Stephanie thought. *At least it's Saturday.*

"Look at that! It's a *winter* sweater," Kimmy maintained. She squinted at the photo. "Those are skiers on it."

D.J. took the picture from her. "No! They're *fall*ing leaves. I'm putting him in November."

"Oh, all right," Kimmy gave in with a sigh.

Stephanie put down her spoon and glanced over at the spread of photographs.

That's when she noticed something surprising. "Hey, these guys are different from the ones you showed me the other day," she observed. "They're all cute. But not as drop-dead gorgeous as the other guys. What happened?"

"Kimmy and I talked," D.J. replied. "We decided to change the theme of the calendar. We've changed it from the hunkiest guys to the twelve most interesting guys at S.F.U."

"Interesting?" Stephanie echoed, not entirely sure what they were getting at.

"These guys are cute, but more than that, they have really amazing personalities," D.J. explained.

Kimmy reached across for a photo and turned it over. On the back, a short biography of the guy had been clipped to it. "See this guy, here? Right now he's doing a series of photographs of babies. He hopes a publisher will buy it someday. Mostly, though, he just likes babies."

D.J. handed her another photo. "This guy volunteers as a firefighter and works at a soup kitchen on weekends."

"And this guy runs a free theater workshop for blind and deaf kids," Kimmy said, showing her a third photo.

"After all," D.J. said, "it's what's inside that counts. I sure learned that lesson the hard way."

"I know *exactly* what you mean," Stephanie said, thinking about J.P. He wasn't the cutest guy she'd ever met, but he was one of the most interesting and the most fun. His personality was what attracted her. What's inside was definitely what counted. And here was the proof—she couldn't get J.P. out of her mind.

Stephanie finished breakfast and started out for Allie's house. She had to talk to her, she realized. She had to try to fix things between them. And if J.P. were there, maybe she could talk to him, too.

Maybe. If he would talk to *her*, that was.

Stephanie walked down her front steps and

came to a sudden stop. Directly across the street, Matt was sitting on his steps with Jennifer.

Jennifer! Stephanie had been counting on not having to see her before Monday.

Jennifer wasn't paying any attention to Stephanie. She and Matt were talking and laughing, and they were holding hands! Either they didn't see Stephanie or they pretended not to.

Stephanie stood still for a moment and thought about it. She could run past them really fast and hope they didn't look up—no, she couldn't. She knew she couldn't just go by them without saying anything. Not after everything that had happened. That would be too cowardly.

Taking a deep breath for courage, she crossed the street and walked up to Matt and Jennifer. "I just want to say I'm sorry—to both of you," Stephanie apologized. "I never expected things to get so crazy."

Jennifer and Matt looked at each other, then back at her. "Maybe I kind of pushed you into it," Jennifer admitted.

Stephanie had to stop her mouth from falling open in shock. Still, she was glad Jennifer said this. Maybe, she thought, it means the game of one-upmanship is finally over.

"Yeah, and at least Jenny and I met," Matt

said. He grinned at Jennifer. She smiled back at him.

"I'm glad something good came out of it," Stephanie said. Then, with a wave, she headed for Allie's house.

Stephanie was relieved when Allie answered the doorbell. Though she wanted to see J.P., she realized she wasn't quite ready for that yet. First, she had to make things right with Allie.

"Hi," Stephanie said to her friend. "I came over because I owe you an apology. Do you think I could come in for a minute?"

Allie looked at her coolly. "Okay," she said at last. "Why don't you come up to my room?"

Allie sat down cross-legged on her bed while Stephanie took the chair across from it.

"I was really rude to you," Stephanie began. "And I didn't even know why I was acting that way."

"That makes two of us," Allie said.

"It wasn't about you and me," Stephanie explained. She took a deep breath. "It was about J.P. actually."

"What?" Allie looked completely confused.

Stephanie nodded. "I finally figured out that I had a thing for J.P. right from the start. Only he didn't fit my idea of what a perfect guy should look like, so I didn't know it at the time. And I didn't even realize I was jealous of you."

"Of me?" Allie asked.

"You get to spend so much time with him. And you and J.P. always have so much fun together."

"He is fun," Allie said. She looked at Stephanie curiously. "You really like him that much?"

Stephanie nodded. "I think he's great. He's so smart and funny. I think his personality actually changed the way I feel about his looks. Now I think he looks really cool." She stopped short, afraid that once again she'd said the wrong thing. "Do *you* like him—I mean, like that?"

"No," Allie said. "I really do think of him as a brother. I couldn't date my brother."

Stephanie relaxed. "Good. I was stupid to be jealous of you. I'm really, really sorry."

"You've said that at least ten times. Stop. It's okay," Allie said, laughing. "And it's fine with me if you want to go out with J.P."

Stephanie shook her head as she got up from the chair. "It doesn't matter if I want to date him. I'm sure he never wants to see me again."

"He did seem kind of bummed last night and

this morning. I think he's pretty upset," Allie said. "But he'll probably get over it in a while."

"Yeah, like when he's back in Paris," Stephanie predicted.

"Maybe you should try to talk to him," Allie suggested.

"I don't think I can," Stephanie said. "I feel too awful. I can't face him." She hugged Allie. "But I'm glad we're friends again."

"Me, too," Allie replied.

Stephanie opened the bedroom door. "I'd better get home," she said. "I didn't tell anyone I was coming over."

She headed down the stairs. Just as she was about to open the front door to let herself out, J.P. stepped into the hallway from the living room.

Stephanie froze. *What is he going to say?* she wondered. *And what could I possibly say that would make this mess any better?* She couldn't think of a single thing. But this might be the last chance she'd ever get to apologize.

"J.P., I'm so sorry about last night," she began. "I never meant to hurt your feelings. I don't think you're a nerd. In fact, I think you're . . . you're very attractive."

Stephanie felt her face turn bright red with

embarrassment. She'd never told a guy she thought he was attractive. It was almost as bad as admitting she had a crush on him. But it was the truth. And considering what had happened, she decided, J.P. needed to hear the truth.

J.P. was quiet for the longest time. Stephanie wondered if he was going to tell her that he never wanted to speak to her again.

Finally he said, "I just left my room a few minutes ago. And I passed Allie's room. I heard what you said to Allie . . . about liking me . . . even if I am a geek."

"No! You're not a geek!" Stephanie had to make him understand. "I told you. I was wrong. *So* wrong. I don't even know how I could have thought that."

J.P.'s voice was hesitant. "You made me feel . . . terrible."

"Don't feel that way," Stephanie begged. "There's no reason for you to. I'm the one who acted terrible. Please, I'll feel even worse than I already do knowing I made you feel bad. Jean-Pierre, you're one of the nicest people I've ever met."

J.P. nodded. The smallest hint of a smile formed at the corners of his mouth. "Maybe I take some getting used to," he said. "Some girls think I'm a rock star, like the ones on the plane. And some girls, like you, think I'm a nerd. You win some, you lose some."

"I am so sorry," Stephanie repeated.

His smile broadened a little. "If you're really sorry, you could make it up to me by taking me out to a movie," he suggested.

"Absolutely!" Stephanie cried. She felt so much lighter. She felt absolutely, totally happy! "Just say when."

"Tonight?"

"Tonight," she repeated. "Okay! Yes! Tonight!"

That evening Stephanie walked out of the multiplex hand in hand with J.P. The movie had been terrific, but that wasn't why she felt so good. Being with J.P. made everything wonderful.

"That movie worked on two levels," he said thoughtfully. "It was as if the terrible storm symbolized the problems between the characters."

"You know, I think that's true," Stephanie agreed. "Like when the wife was fighting with her husband. The storm was crashing so loudly through the trees outside."

"Exactly," he said. "They are parallel."

As J.P. talked about the movie, Stephanie noticed Jennifer and some of her friends standing by the escalator. She saw some of them glance at her and snicker among themselves. Stephanie knew they were snickering at J.P. and his unique look.

It didn't bother her. Stephanie smiled at them and waved. She liked being seen with J.P., someone who was interesting and funny and really nice. Let them think what they liked. They'd never know what they were missing.

"Stephanie," J.P. said as they neared the food court. "How about some dessert."

They sat down at a table at a pastry shop. Stephanie ordered a piece of chocolate cake. J.P. ordered an eclair.

"You know this isn't good," J.P. said after the waitress left.

"Oh, I know," Stephanie said apologetically. "I know American food will never be as good as French—"

"The food's not the problem," J.P. cut her off with a laugh. "You are."

I am? Stephanie thought with a sinking heart. *Now what have I done?*

"I have too good a time when I am with you," J.P. explained. "It will be hard to go home in a month."

131

"I'm not going to think about that," Stephanie said. "I want to enjoy your company while you're here. Besides, we can always write to each other."

"We can send videos, too," he suggested. "It will be good practice for us, for when we become hotshot news reporters. I will open my show saying, 'Here is J.P., with all the latest news from Paris."

"Mine will start, 'Reporting from San Francisco, Stephanie Tanner!'"

They laughed, then J.P. drew Stephanie close and kissed her. Her eyes slid shut and she returned his kiss. Everything inside her tingled with excitement.

"Wow!" she said after they broke apart. "I started this whole thing looking for the perfect mail-order brother. And what I got was a perfect mail-order boyfriend!"

FULL HOUSE™
Club Stephanie

Summer is here and Stephanie is ready for some fun!

A brand-new miniseries! Collect all three books.

#1 Fun, Sun, and Flamingoes
#2 Fireworks and Flamingoes
#3 Flamingo Revenge

-All Now Available-

Based on the hit Warner Bros. TV series!

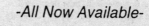

A MINSTREL® BOOK

Published by Pocket Books

FULL HOUSE™
Michelle

#5: THE GHOST IN MY CLOSET 53573-0/$3.99

#6: BALLET SURPRISE 53574-9/$3.99

#7: MAJOR LEAGUE TROUBLE 53575-7/$3.99

#8: MY FOURTH-GRADE MESS 53576-5/$3.99

#9: BUNK 3, TEDDY, AND ME 56834-5/$3.99

#10: MY BEST FRIEND IS A MOVIE STAR!
(Super Edition) 56835-3/$3.99

#11: THE BIG TURKEY ESCAPE 56836-1/$3.99

#12: THE SUBSTITUTE TEACHER 00364-X/$3.99

#13: CALLING ALL PLANETS 00365-8/$3.99

#14: I'VE GOT A SECRET 00366-6/$3.99

#15: HOW TO BE COOL 00833-1/$3.99

#16: THE NOT-SO-GREAT OUTDOORS 00835-8/$3.99

#17: MY HO-HO-HORRIBLE CHRISTMAS 00836-6/$3.99

MY AWESOME HOLIDAY FRIENDSHIP BOOK
(An Activity Book) 00840-4/$3.99

FULL HOUSE MICHELLE OMNIBUS 02181-8/$6.99

#18: MY ALMOST PERFECT PLAN 00837-4/$3.99

#19: APRIL FOOLS 01729-2/$3.99

A MINSTREL® BOOK
Published by Pocket Books

Simon & Schuster Mail Order Dept. BWB
200 Old Tappan Rd., Old Tappan, N.J. 07675

Please send me the books I have checked above. I am enclosing $_____ (please add $0.75 to cover the postage and handling for each order. Please add appropriate sales tax). Send check or money order--no cash or C.O.D.'s please. Allow up to six weeks for delivery. For purchase over $10.00 you may use VISA: card number, expiration date and customer signature must be included.

Name _____

Address _____

City _____ State/Zip _____

VISA Card # _____ Exp.Date _____

Signature _____

1033-26

FULL HOUSE™

SISTERS

A brand-new series starring Stephanie AND Michelle!

#1 Two On The Town

Stephanie and Michelle find themselves
in the big city—and in big trouble!

(Coming in mid-November 1998)

#2 One Boss Too Many

Stephanie and Michelle think camp will be major fun.
If only these two sisters were getting along!

(Coming in mid-December 1998)

When sisters get together...expect the unexpected!

A MINSTREL® BOOK

Published by Pocket Books

2012

FULL HOUSE Stephanie™

PHONE CALL FROM A FLAMINGO	88004-7/$3.99
THE BOY-OH-BOY NEXT DOOR	88121-3/$3.99
TWIN TROUBLES	88290-2/$3.99
HIP HOP TILL YOU DROP	88291-0/$3.99
HERE COMES THE BRAND NEW ME	89858-2/$3.99
THE SECRET'S OUT	89859-0/$3.99
DADDY'S NOT-SO-LITTLE GIRL	89860-4/$3.99
P.S. FRIENDS FOREVER	89861-2/$3.99
GETTING EVEN WITH THE FLAMINGOES	52273-6/$3.99
THE DUDE OF MY DREAMS	52274-4/$3.99
BACK-TO-SCHOOL COOL	52275-2/$3.99
PICTURE ME FAMOUS	52276-0/$3.99
TWO-FOR-ONE CHRISTMAS FUN	53546-3/$3.99
THE BIG FIX-UP MIX-UP	53547-1/$3.99
TEN WAYS TO WRECK A DATE	53548-X/$3.99
WISH UPON A VCR	53549-8/$3.99
DOUBLES OR NOTHING	56841-8/$3.99
SUGAR AND SPICE ADVICE	56842-6/$3.99
NEVER TRUST A FLAMINGO	56843-4/$3.99
THE TRUTH ABOUT BOYS	00361-5/$3.99
CRAZY ABOUT THE FUTURE	00362-3/$3.99
MY SECRET ADMIRER	00363-1/$3.99
BLUE RIBBON CHRISTMAS	00830-7/$3.99
THE STORY ON OLDER BOYS	00831-5/$3.99
MY THREE WEEKS AS A SPY	00832-3/$3.99
NO BUSINESS LIKE SHOW BUSINESS	01725-X/$3.99

Available from Minstrel® Books Published by Pocket Books